NIGHTTIME RESCUE

How long they'd been asleep, Chris didn't know, before the sound of the rushing water and the rain was shattered by the screaming, crashing sound of a car skidding on the road, banging into the guard-rail, and slamming into the trees off to the right.

Chris sat up, his hand wildly clutching at Jock's arm. "Paw-paw, what was that?"

"Ain't sure, boy. 'Pears somebody come off'n the road goin' ninety to nothin'."

"Help!" a man's voice called. "Anybody, some-body, come help me!"

The Gitaway Box

HILARY MILTON

Printed in the United States of America
Library of Congress Catalog Number: 79-57211
ISBN: 0-89191-243-6

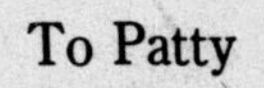
To Patty

1 ....

The old man sat on the edge of the narrow, rumpled bed in the room semidarkened by the elastic dusk of daylight saving time. With slow, faltering motions, he massaged the boy's shoulders, rough fingers attempting to be gentle, aged muscles fighting back the quivers.

Outside, the warm spring evening hinted of life, of warmer days to come, of leaves and grass turning green, of a tomorrow that promised all kinds of exciting fulfillment. Inside, the leftover aroma of greenhouse flowers already picked and carefully arranged in a special manner provided its own saturating contradiction.

The boy on the bed stirred and sniffled. There was no

more crying left in him—only the aftermath of sobs. "Paw-paw, what's death?"

The old man's hand stopped, then moved again slowly. "Death, boy? Why, I reckon death's everything life ain't."

That didn't tell it right but Jock didn't know any better way of saying it. He'd thought on it, too, in the long hours since that police officer in the black car with the blue letters and red light came to tell him how it happened—how Andy and Stella had come up hard on the truck without taillights in the rain, and how the car behind them hadn't stopped, either. And how death had chosen the middle vehicle, sparing the man in the truck and the kid in the car behind. Just Andy and Stella.

That wasn't how it was supposed to be. The old man goes before the young, the father does not go till the child is more than child. Order didn't matter, though—not now. Stella dead. Andy dead. And the boy left with the ageless question and the aging grandfather. Nothing else.

The boy stirred without purpose. "Then I guess mommy's got her dishwasher, and daddy's got that hunting rifle he was aiming to buy, come hunting season. Reckon?"

"I reckon."

The total confusion, cleared and simplified by a dishwasher and a rifle. Jock swallowed hard and stiffened his arm against the tremor. He stared down at the tousled hair on the tear-wet pillow, looking through what he saw and back and back, to another little boy and another time, and it was the same—the same even face, the waves in black, mussed hair, and he was telling his son, Andy, about Old Dawg—how Old Dawg had got mistook for a fox by a city fellow had no business hunting, anyway, and got shot. No dishwasher and rifle perfection for Andy—just a gone pet and no more rabbit jumping.

He turned away from the boy and looked out through the open window toward the different shades of gray shadows that were trees and houses and boxed-in little yards hardly worthy of the name. The tight little community of close-set neighbors who barely knew the occupants of the houses on either side was like a set-apart world, with him and the boy now having no contact. Three had stopped in to say their sorries about Andy and Stella, one bringing a store-bought cake and a plate of sliced ham, another putting a baking tin of salad in the refrigerator and saying it doesn't matter if the tin gets thrown out, and the third bringing a box of cookies then stopping in the front room long enough to rearrange the artificial flowers Stella had always kept on the mantel. But none brought the thing you needed most, coffee to moisten dry lips or milk that would go down a little boy's throat when nothing else would. All together, they lived in the thing called a subdivision; and not one really knew the other.

And not one asked the main question.

Jock dared not think about it now.

He caught the upper edge of the wrinkled sheet and tugged it straight. Tenderly, then, he brought it up and around the boy's shoulder, letting it rest there, not so much to ward off the cool night as to suggest a vague and uncertain comfort. "Boy, you sleep now," he said. "Close your eyes and tell God all your troubles—he'll listen. Paw-paw's got things to see to."

"I'll try."

The old man got up slowly, stood there for a moment looking down. "Night, son."

"G'night—" But the word *Paw-paw* got caught on a hard sob.

It was because Paw-paw had called him *son*, and they both knew it.

Jock walked into the short hallway, closing the boy's door against the lights he would have to turn on. He took two short steps to the bedroom that Andy and Stella had shared. He felt for the switch, flicked it on, and stood there for a moment scanning the way the room looked. It was just as she had made it up three days earlier, the morning of the day before the night they took the ride and didn't come home. The pillows on the bed were halfway rolled up under the flowery spread. Jock didn't know why it was done that way—a pillow was for putting your head on at night, and rolling it up that way didn't seem the way to do it—but that's how Stella thought it ought to be. And the dresser top was dignified, with the little blue box of whatevers there in the middle, an oval-shaped hand mirror to one side, and a comb and brush to the other. A small gold-framed picture of Chris when he was a baby was at one end and some kind of sweet water or perfume sprayer opposite.

In the far corner of the room, jammed in between the bed and the wall, was a narrow chest of drawers of a finish that differed from the dresser, bed, and stand. Its top was totally bare except for the one item Jock would never forget. In Korea, while he was in the hospital recovering from the wound that just missed shattering his shoulder, Andy had carved the little wooden stand. He had shaped it like a pistol, butt-end down and barrel pointing up, and at the very uppermost part of it he'd put the bullet they took from his body. A reminder, he'd called it, of how close death could come without taking you along.

Jock turned away.

Somewhere—he knew—somewhere inside one of those drawers he would find when the time came to look for it a cigar box stuffed full of special trinkets and papers, of souvenirs and tokens, and no matter their value, they would all be carefully sorted into tight little rubber band-bound bundles, each clearly marked. The box was certain to be there, Jock knew, its presence a carry-over from the time when he and Martha and their three girls and Andy had shared a cropper's shack three miles out from Reader's Gap. There'd been precious little room for sleeping, let along for keeping worthless little treasures a boy would cling to. So Andy had found himself a cigar box just the right size to put in the gap between the fireplace and the window, and in it he'd kept the things prized most—the fine-line fishing cord tightly wrapped around its cork, the postcard picture of that Lindbergh fellow who flew across the ocean, the red and white Vote-for-FDR pin, two gnarled buckeyes, and the battered cover and remnant pieces of an old Bible. Through all his growing-up years, the contents changed now and again, but the idea remained.

Whatever had to be known about Andy now would be in papers in the cigar box, stuck away in the corner of one of those drawers. Jock would find it. But not tonight.

He flicked off the light and felt his way through the hall toward the living room and the small dining room, and the even smaller kitchen. The dusk had mostly gone now, but just enough remained to let Jock go without lights to the stove where the half-empty percolator sat. Absently, he sniffed at the spout. Cold as it was, it was still strong—and heavy enough to blot out the lingering scent of the flowers. He poured most of what was left into the unwashed mug on the counter. Carefully, he carried it toward the front door, bumping the screen open with his foot, and made his way across to the two concrete steps. At the edge of the porch nearest the post he sat down and dangled his feet till his heels touched the little bit of a sidewalk. He leaned back and to the side, letting the post support him, and he placed the mug on the concrete floor. Now in the darkness, his slumped body blended into the shadows.

And now it was over and done with and the one son he had helped bring into the world was dead—wife dead, too—and left in the hollow house were the old man who had lived too much of life and the young boy who had lived none of it. The direct link between them was no more, and the span of time separating them was far too great.

Jock swigged at the cold coffee then breathed heavily, diluting the acid bitterness. There were no tears left, nothing but the dry, twisted thought of never-forever, the absolute silence of space no longer taken by a son no longer there, only the living echo in the form of a nine year old. Jock had cried hard tears when the doctor told him twenty-two years ago that Jean Ann would never be right in the head again and that the time would come when he and Martha would have to put her in the state hospital. And his eyes had moistened three years earlier, when he had stood by the mound of broken red dirt at the graveyard and watched as they lowered Martha's body into its final resting place. But no tears now.

He rubbed the back of his hand across his forehead. When Martha died he had told Mary Lou, his oldest daughter, and Jessica, his youngest—and he guessed he told Andy, too, but that didn't matter now—that all he cared about was one more trip, his own, to the plot next to hers. Patiently, he had waited.

Now that trip would have to be postponed.

A plane made a slow arc overhead, its little red and green lights blinking and its landing lights cutting through the early night as it moved toward the airport by the river—the National, he thought that's what Andy had said. Never made sense to him, having a noisy airport right there across the water from the United States capital. He watched it out of sight.

Jock swallowed the last of the coffee, then leaned back

still farther, till his head touched the rough and now dew-dampened porch post. He sighed and thought about the long, long way from Arlington to Bucksville, Alabama, the states and cities in between, the day-long-night-long train ride he'd taken to get here only a month before—the journey he hadn't wanted to make but had made, anyway, because he'd promised he'd do it as soon as Andy and Stella had a house and a bed he could sleep on, and could send him the fare because he had too little living-on money, none at all for traveling.

It had not been planned for this. It had not been intended as a journey toward guardianship. Yet here he was in a world he did not know, and there they were in a world to which every man goes as a stranger. And there the boy was, restless and alone.

Enough to make a lesser man doubt the wisdom of God. But in spite of all the things he questioned, he couldn't doubt God. He had watched prolonged rains fall on cotton bolls, ripe for the picking, till the white was mud-splattered and rotting. He had seen drouth-stunted corn turned harvesttime brown in July, with silk brittle crisp and ears of fruit no bigger than bird eggs. And during those few years before and through the war, when he had worked in the iron ore mines because crops didn't pay and mucking did, he had seen a working slate hanging wall come crashing-crumbling down on three drillmen. He had stood by, watching liveliness yield to lifelessness in Jean Ann. And he had knelt at Martha's grave. And this very afternoon he had followed the hearse in the funeral director's car.

Through those years he had often doubted himself. But not once God.

He closed his eyes, sensed the numbing agony throughout his body, the nerve-tight tremors in his legs, the heaviness of his arms and hands. The urge for sleep pressed down upon him and bits and pieces of thought came and went. It was Andy's sixteenth birthday and while the single-barrel twelve gauge wasn't new it was accurate. And it was April 1951 and the telegram came through the mail because there were no telegram deliveries out where they lived. The telegram said that Andy had been shot bad, and a week later the letter came from the Red Cross lady, saying Andy was alive and recovering from the wound. And it was Andy coming home and getting married, then not knowing what to do with himself, getting caught repairing motors for that automobile theft ring and having to spend five years on probation. It was Andy trying to be a good mechanic but not having any luck getting a job because nobody wanted to trust him after that probation business, and it was finally Andy leaving home and coming a-way up to Arlington, Virginia, where nobody knew him, and he and Stella making a fresh start. It was Mary Lou packing up with that banjo-playing Texas fellow called Marty Jenkins and going someplace west, where he rode herd on cows in the winter and played country music in the spring. It was Jessica and her brood of seven and that husband R.T.—and it was somebody crying out, somebody screaming out in the night—this night, not one long ago in the past.

"Mommy! Daddy! Mommy-daddy! Mommy-daddy-mommy-daddy-mommy!"

The sound broke through the stillness of the tight little subdivision in Arlington, Virginia, just across from the capital of the United States. And old Jock started at the sound, started and tripped, caught himself against the porch post, fumbled for the screen door, crashed through it, knocking it half off its hinges and going on, stumbled over a chair and banged against the wall, kicked a magazine rack out of his way and bulled through the short hall to the boy's room. Inside it, he caught his foot on a small throw rug and rumbled uncertainly forward. He hit the edge of the bed Chris was lying on and sprawled halfway upon it.

And as he did, wiry little arms reached out and clutched at him, tight fingers dug into his neck, and a hot face buried itself against his chest. His own arms trembled and his hands shook as Jock caught the boy to him, held him close, pressed his own face down upon the tousled hair. He knew tears then. "God love you, boy, don't holler so. Don't holler. We'll make it," he said, "we'll make it, me and you."

2 ....

Jock kept Chris home from school Friday, the day following the funeral, and they spent it and the weekend staying out in the yard where the sunshine was, away from the hidden secrets of dresser drawers and closet doors, out of the rooms where the aroma of flowers was still thick and the silence was heavy. They cut the grass and raked the lawn, trimmed the shrubbery and carefully worked the dirt at the roots of the azaleas Stella had put so much store by. Wherever Jock went, Chris dogged his trail, elbow to elbow while the mowing was done, knee against knee when they squatted to work the dirt. Once while they were examining a bush limb that had been broken half off by the mower, the boy said, "Reckon they're in heaven now." Jock had pressed the tip of the limb, then squeezed it hard when he had said, "Yeah, I reckon." And again when they went inside to get cold water from the milk bottle Jock had put in the refrigerator, the boy had said, "Mommy had a pitcher once. She used it for water, but I broke it. I wish I hadn't—she liked it better than anything." Jock nodded and said, "Lots o' things get broke."

Jock wasn't much for cooking and he'd never cared for sandwiches. That was one of the things he'd disliked most about those years in the mines—no hot meals. But Sunday afternoon it came to him that maybe the boy'd do better if he had a picnic in that place—what'd they call it?—community park?—well, whatever it was, down the street. So he put together two cheese and two peanut-butter and jelly sandwiches and he poured two fruit jars almost full of milk. They walked down and found a quiet place away from the swings and seesaws, over near the shallow stream that wound through the land. They sat at a dirty table where the last people had spilled catsup and didn't wipe it up—they covered it with a newspaper sheet—and they ate silently. Jock noticed the boy seemed to swallow hard while he was chewing, as if his mind went somewhere else and what he thought about made a kind of fist in his throat. But he didn't let on he saw.

They'd no more than finished when a small gray squirrel stopped on a tree branch just above them and scolded away, as if they were interlopers in his private domain. Jock clucked softly to him, then casually thumbed a crust toward the tree trunk. The little animal scurried down to clutch it and scurried back up. "Taking it to his little'uns," Jock said.

Chris looked up toward the tree branch and slowly dug the back of his hand into his eye. "Or maybe storing it somewhere."

Jock meant for the boy to slide down the sliding board or take a turn at swinging, but Chris wouldn't move two feet from him. So when it began to turn shadowy dusk they trudged back toward the subdivision and home.

Monday morning Jock got up early and cooked a pan of bacon and scrambled four eggs. When it was ready, he roused the boy and called him to the kitchen. "Best you go back to school today," he said. "No sense missing any more."

"No sense going to school—now, nothing to go for. And don't anybody care."

"Paw-paw cares. Now, you eat. Got to eat to stay strong and healthy. Anybody goes to school hungry can't do his work. Can't learn readin' and writin' and his numbers."

"I can already read and write, and numbers don't help you do anything." But he finally sat down and began to eat his breakfast. "Paw-paw," he said once between bites, "did you go to college?"

For the first time since that night they heard about Andy and Stella, Jock smiled. "Boy, I never made it through the fourth grade—that's the grade you're in now, ain't it?" He spooned up bacon and eggs on the blade of a dull knife and put it in his mouth. "Schoolin' wasn't near as important when I was a shaver as it is now."

"Not important to me—now," the boy said.

"Never mind that." Jock tried to make it sound firm but not gruff. "No more'n two little weeks til school's out." He looked straight at Chris, then. "Your ma and pa wouldn't like you quitting."

"But they're not here."

"But they're looking," Jock said. "Wherever heaven is, they're looking down, seeing what you do. Don't ever forget that."

The boy looked straight at him, tears forming in his eyes. "Maybe they can't see so good."

"They can see good," Jock said. "Now you eat that bacon and them eggs, and Paw-paw'll walk you to school."

The boy took a deep breath and wiped the back of his hand across his eyes. For a moment he seemed to want to say something else but he did not. He touched the tip of his tongue to his lips and swallowed hard, then he slowly turned his attention to the plate of food before him. "I wish I could see them, too, though," he said between bites.

Jock cleared his throat and took a burning sip of hot coffee.

While the boy was dressing himself for school, Jock piled the dishes in the sink. He'd get to them later, let 'em soak now and wouldn't take much more than wiping off. Never had seemed right to him, a man washing dishes.

The route to school was a short one but Chris walked slowly, now and again zigzagging across the sidewalk, pausing once to brush his foot over a silvery spider web on the side of a boxwood plant. Once, half a block from the school, he stopped and turned back to Jock. "I don't want to go. I want to stay with you."

Jock did not know all the fancy words people used when they talked about little boys, but he sensed the fear in Chris. He put his hand on the boy's shoulder, touched the nape of his neck. "Paw-paw's got some things to do. You go on to school while I get done what I've gotta, then I'll meet you right here on the corner and we'll go to that drugstore up the road. Get some ice cream, maybe." He led the boy to the corner where the guard was.

When the guard said to cross over and Chris went with the two or three others who were also waiting, Jock stood and watched after him till he was in the building. He waited there till the bell rang, to make sure he didn't come running out.

Back at the house, Jock did what he had postponed for four days. He opened the drawers in the dresser one at a time, deliberately avoiding the socks and the underwear and the shirts carefully placed there, looking for one thing. He found it just as he had been so certain he would—stuck back in the next to the bottom drawer. It wasn't the same old cigar box of long ago, but it was a box much like that one, with the brand name scrawled over and the word *KEEP* printed in large, black uneven letters.

He took it out, shut the drawer, and sat down on the edge of the bed. Slowly he put on his glasses and lifted the lid. He found four separate bundles, each held together by rubber bands, and each carefully labeled: army and court papers, house and insurance, marriage license and birth certificate, misc. letters. Jock extracted only the house and insurance packet and slowly closed the box. It was not till he put it back in the drawer that he noticed another packet lying loose inside. The label on it said, "bills, payments, and checks." That, he knew, he'd have to look at, too.

Half an hour later, still sitting in the bedroom, he had all the details he needed, some he did not want. Andy had less than two hundred dollars in the bank. He had no life insurance at all, the nearest thing to it being six G.I. premium notices and a final one saying canceled. The only real insurance was fire coverage for the house. There was not even a policy to cover burial costs. The washing machine and the television set and even some of the furniture was time bought, with most of the balance left to pay. The house had a first mortgage and something called a second trust that Jock didn't understand—although he figured it meant more owed. And nothing for the boy.

Jock got up and walked into the little kitchen and stood there at the sink, looking out the small window. Not his way of doing, that much he'd take a oath on. Never had much, never owned much, but he never owed a debt and never meant to. And he didn't mean for Andy's name to be blotted over in death, either.

The telephone rang, its jangle shattering the total silence of the house. Jock turned toward the extension hung on the wall and looked at it. The ring came a second time, a third, a fourth, a fifth. He had meant not to answer, but it looked like whoever the caller was had no intention of letting him off that easy. After the seventh ring, he walked over and picked it up. "Yep," he said, "Jock Ransome."

"Mr. Ransome," the man at the other end said, "Paul Creighton—of Creighton Funeral Home. I hate to call so soon, about such a delicate matter."

Jock took dead aim over the phone. "If you're callin' about money for the buryin'," he said, "I don't have it. But I'll get it. Count on it, mister, no Ransome debt's goin' unpaid long as I got a breath left in me. But don't call me no more. Just count on gettin' it," and he hung up.

He spent a few minutes rinsing the dishes, then he left them to drip dry in the rack. He went to the room he'd been using, picked up his coat and hat, jammed the last $27.51 he could call his own into his pants pocket, and went out.

He caught a bus and rode the three miles to Proctor's Used Cars, Incorporated, where Andy had been mechanic. After listening to Mr. Proctor repeat his sorries for the third time, he asked if Andy had any pay coming. Mr. Proctor hesitated a moment then said, "Well, there were those last two days before the accident, wasn't much, $39.93 after taxes."

"I'll take it," Jock said.

"Well, I don't know, the law's funny about a dead man's money," Mr. Proctor said.

"It's to pay Andy's just debts, an' I'm his pa. I don't aim for my boy's debts to go unpaid."

Mr. Proctor still wasn't sure, but in the end he went to the cash register and took out two twenties. "Here," he said, "if you'll sign for it." He pushed forward a blank sheet of paper.

Jock wrote in his scrawling hand "Andrew Ransome's pay, taken in full"—and signed his name. He fished a nickel and two pennies from his pocket and handed them to the man.

"You don't need to do that."

"I don't want no more, no less than he's got comin'," Jock said. "Good day to you."

Next, he caught another bus and rode in another direction toward the Dominion Trust Bank. Near the intersection of Wilson Boulevard and Fairfax Drive he got off and walked the remaining three blocks. At the revolving door, he stood for a moment staring at it before going through. Inside, he didn't know who he wanted to see, so he asked for the man in charge of house loans. "That'd be Mr. Haley." The girl pointed to a man in his late twenties.

Jock looked at Mr. Haley. "Don't care to do business with young whipper-snappers." He walked over to the other side of the bank, where a man in his sixties was bent over a stack of papers. Jock cleared his throat.

"I come to turn this in and get my boy's come-back." He put the house mortgage papers on top of the others the man was studying.

The man looked up. "Mr. Haley handles house loans," he said, "but—turn it in? Come-back?" He unfolded the paper.

"Yes, sir," Jock said. "My boy, that's him," and he reached across and put his finger on the name, "Andrew Ransome—Andy, I called him. Him and his wife got themselves killed in a car last week—maybe you read about it, it was in the papers—and ain't nobody to pay it off for him. Nobody left but me and his kid. Figured to turn it in and get whatever come-back's due him." He looked at the man. "Didn't catch your name," he said.

"Braddock, Timothy Braddock. But there's nothing I can do." He studied the document carefully. "I didn't know your son," he said, "but I recall reading about the accident. I'm very sorry."

"Terrible thing," Jock said, "leavin' a kid and nobody to see to him but a wore-out old man. And leavin' money owin' all over town. That's how come I need the come-back. Ain't right for a man to go to his final restin' place with debts hangin' over his grave. I mean to clear his name. The name of Ransome ain't ever been clouded over by debts, and it ain't going to be."

Mr. Braddock stared up at Jock and there was a glimmer of understanding in his eyes. "I'm sure he left a will."

"No such thing. Reckon he didn't figure to die just yet. Young-uns don't never figure to die, always thinking it's us old'uns that'll go first."

"If he died intestate, then," Mr. Braddock said, "the

court will have to make proper disposal. It will have to be handled according to the laws of the state."

"Don't know about your laws in this state," Jock said. "Don't care about 'em, either. But I mean to clear the name of Ransome o' debts."

Mr. Braddock nodded slowly. Jock sat down and they talked more about the papers and about the funeral home bills and all the things Andy had bought on time-payment plans. After a while, Mr. Braddock called Paul Creighton at the Creighton Funeral Home. When he hung up he said, "This whole thing's pretty irregular."

"Gettin' killed this way, him an his wife, and leaving a kid's irregular, too, I guess."

"Yes. Well," Mr. Braddock said, "we here at the bank will see to the house. It will take a while, with the court procedure, and we can't give you a re—a come-back now. But if you give Mr. Creighton fifty dollars, he'll wait for the balance till the mortgage is settled."

Jock thought about the $39.93 he had gotten from Mr. Proctor and the little cash of his own. "I'll get him the fifty. You tell him I'll do it. And if there's any extra charge for waiting a spell, you can give him that, too, out of the come-back."

Jock got up and bid Mr. Braddock a good day. "Terrible thing," he said just before he left, "the way young folks get themselves head over heels in debt and no way out in a pinch."

Out in the open air once more, he asked directions of the policeman checking meters, then walked the six blocks down and around the second corner to the

Statewide Furniture and Appliance Mart. With hardly a glance at the hodgepodge of beds and radios and electric irons and television sets and washing machines in the front window, he pushed the door open. To the smiling young lady who asked, "Can I help you," he said, "I want to see your head man."

"If you mean Mr. Sampsen, he's back at the desk."

"I thank you ma'am," Jock said. He worked through the crowded chairs and lamps and endless tables to the little partitioned-off place marked Office by black letters painted on a white signboard. He stopped at the desk and took a manila card from his coat pocket and put it in front of the man.

Mr. Sampsen looked at it, then turned to Jock. "Can I help you?"

"My boy bought some things from you on account. He's dead now and there ain't nobody to pay. Thought maybe you'd better come pick 'em up."

Mr. Sampsen didn't seem to know what to do. He looked at the payment card, looked again at Jock, got up and walked over to a big file cabinet, opened one of the drawers, stopped and came back and read the name once more, then finally went to the file drawer and pulled out a large folder. He returned to his desk and spread the notes before him. "Let's see, Andrew Ransome, age 38, employed by Proctor Used Cars, wife named Stella." He stopped and looked at Jock. "Maybe she can pick up the payments."

"She was killed with my boy."

"Hmm, hmm, hmm," the man said. He shook his

head. "No more than nine weeks ago he bought over $700 worth of merchandise. Paid down fifty, owes twenty-five a month for thirty months."

"That's him," Jock said. "And like I say, ain't nobody to pay."

"Maybe there's money in his estate." The man looked up.

"No estate or whatever. Nothing for you to do but come get it."

The man shook his head. "Hmm, hmm, hmm. The trouble with time payments, you can't ever sell used goods for what you have in them, no matter how new." He looked hard at Jock. "What about insurance? Surely he had some insurance. And his house, that's worth something."

"I done turned it in. The boy's come-back from it won't no more'n pay for his burying—him and his wife's."

"And you're sure you don't want to assume it—I mean, it's fine merchandise, the price he was paying."

"I'm certain it's mighty fine," Jock said, "but I'm broker'n a hant. But he's took care of it, him and Stella—good as new, come see it for yourself."

Mr. Sampsen took a deep breath and made a noise sighing it out. "Well, I suppose there's nothing else to do but repossess it." He sighed and made a noise again. "That's the bad thing about this time payment business, Mr. Ransome. You never know who's going to pay up and who's not. Don't know but what we ought to put insurance on every account over a hundred dollars."

"I understand," Jock said. "Must be pretty hard, separating honest folks from deadbeats. But you can stake your life on one thing," he went on. "My boy wasn't a deadbeat; he'd of paid up. Trouble now is, he can't."

"And that's the pity of it," Mr. Sampsen said. He turned toward a side door and hollered through it for somebody named Henry.

A big fellow dressed in dark brown trousers and slip-on green shirt appeared. "Yeah?"

"Got a repossess," Mr. Sampsen said.

"A big load like the last one, I guess," the man called Henry said.

Mr. Sampsen threw a quick frowning glance at Jock. "Not so big. Washing machine and a television set and a hollywood bed set—and a sofa."

"That's the settee you're meaning," Jock nodded.

"Better take the van, Henry, after lunch."

"Mister," Jock looked at Sampsen, "care if I ride out with him? I can show him where the house is."

"Good idea," Mr. Sampsen said. "Go around back and sit in the van—that's a big blue truck with our name in white letters on the side."

"Much obliged," Jock said. "Sorry to put you out so."

Mr. Sampsen vaguely waved his hand in the air. "Well, that's how it is with credit retailing."

On the ride out, Jock sat in the front seat with the fellow called Henry. Two helpers rode in the back. Jock said nothing, just sat staring through the smeared-over windshield.

As the truck cleared the heavy traffic at Wilson and Glebe, Henry lit a cigarette. "Looks like you bit off more'n you could chew, old man."

Jock bit back the words he wanted to use. "Nope."

"Nope," Henry echoed, "nobody ever does. Always the store's fault; stuff ain't worth the price, they say after they use it awhile. Oughtn't of bought it in the first place."

Jock stared out the window. "Wasn't me that bought; it was my boy, Andy."

"And he run out," Henry said.

"Might say that," Jock said, "'cept it ain't true. Him and his wife got killed last week, car wreck."

Henry blew a thick cloud of smoke that swirled across the dashboard. "Hey, was that the car got caught between a truck and a hotrod—bet it was. I saw that picture in the paper. What a mess. Was that your boy?"

"That was him."

"What a mess," Henry repeated. "Way that thing was stove in, seemed like they was burning rubber. Tore'em up pretty bad, too, I reckon. I mean, you could tell from the picture couldn't anybody get out of that mess alive." He flipped the cigarette through the open side window. "Me, I like to drive fast as the next one—not in this truck, it'd bust the block makin' fifty—but I got a '59 Chev'll do ninety-eight in a half mile—you know, bored and shaved, two carbs, four on the floor. But I'll not let'er out around here.

"I seen a car once," Henry continued, "doing eighty-five, maybe ninety, had a blowout on the interstate—you know where the interstate route is, five or six miles out—crazy thing turned over five times. Driver was pinned between the door and the seat. When they got to him, deader'n a doornail, his foot was still clamping down on the gas. Guess your boy didn't live to say what happened."

Jock looked out the window, stared at the houses. "I don't know. I wasn't with him."

"Guess it was a good thing," Henry said. "Terrible thing, seeing your own kin tore up by a car."

When they got to the house Jock climbed out and went straight to the front door. He unlocked it and propped open the screen. He showed them where the items were, then stood out of the way while they picked them up. One of the men bumped the door with the television set and put a scratch in it. And while the other two were carrying the washing machine they let water trail all the way across the little rug in the living room. Stella wouldn't have liked that. The way she kept the place, she'd have made them clean it up before they left.

Jock said nothing, just stood there, watching.

It took them half an hour to make the pickups, and Jock wondered while they were at it how long Stella and Andy had spent looking, then making up their minds to buy, then figuring out how they could pay for it, then finally putting up $50 and signing for the balance. Took a summer to make a crop of cotton, one night of rain at the wrong time to spoil it.

When the final item was on the truck and the tailgate swung in place, Jock handed Henry the brown payment card. "Write on it that you got the contraptions."

"That's for Mr. Sampsen to do," Henry said.

"Mr. Sampsen ain't here," Jock said, "and you working for him, your word's good as his now."

In the end Henry itemized the repossessed pieces, but he hesitated about signing his own name. "Be all right if I put down the name of the company?"

"Just so long as it's proper done," Jock said.

Henry looked at him once, then wrote in his scrawling hand, "Statewide Furniture and Appliance Mart"—stopping often to look at the truck for the spelling. When he'd done that, he handed the card back to Jock and turned toward the truck.

"One more thing, young fella."

Henry looked back.

"Don't never talk to folks about their dead kin the way you done to me." And while Henry stood there saying nothing, Jock turned his back on him and slowly made his way into the house.

Alone once more, he went across the hall to the bedroom where the mattress and box springs had been standing on little stubby legs. He put one hand on the doorframe and leaned heavily against it. One of the men—Jock didn't know which, and it didn't matter now, nothing really mattered now except the boy—one of them had pulled off the sheets and the pillows and the bedspread and piled them carelessly in the chair stuck away in the corner. Stella'd been proud of that spread, found it in one of those Goodwill Industry places, she said. Some crippled fellow had spent a lot of time making it back like it was at first, with the raised red roses with green stems and leaves across the top where it covered the pillows. Always folded it just so at night, she did, so the roses and stems were not bent or covered over in any way. The fellow'd dumped it on the chair, though, and one of the stems was bent; looked like the rose petals had been smashed and spread out too.

Jock rubbed both eyes with the knuckles of his free hand and turned away.

He looked at the electric clock hung out in the hall, then, and suddenly he remembered Chris. Fifteen minutes, that's all he had, just fifteen minutes to walk all the way to that corner. He lifted one tired foot and flexed the ankle, then did the same to the other. He knew the aches that would be in his tiring legs tonight, all that walking and standing. But never mind it now, had to go, had to meet the boy.

That's what he'd promised.

He hurried and he crossed two streets against the light when no cars were coming and he had to walk faster than he should have down the little incline just before he got to the last corner and he had to stop there and lean against the light pole to catch his breath. But he was waiting, just as he'd told the boy he would, when they let out across the street.

Jock had forgotten what Chris had worn to school that morning, but it made no difference. The moment the boy got to the door he turned searching eyes toward the place where Jock had left him. Almost instantly Jock knew he'd been spotted. Chris darted around a knot of boys and girls ambling toward the intersection and ran the hundred feet to the curb, first at the point when the crossing guard gave the signal.

"I was hoping you'd be here." He grabbed for Jock's hand and pressed himself against the worn old body.

"Told you I'd be." Jock caught the boy's chin and raised it slowly, saw the telltale after-streaks of tears. "You been cryin' again." He said it softly, though.

"Didn't mean to, but teacher gave us this, something about the night program for parents."

Jock took the paper and jammed it in his pocket without glancing at it. "We'll see to that later." He turned around, arm about the boy's shoulder, and they started home.

When they reached the house, Jock had a notion to sprawl on the grass and just sit in the yard a spell. But before he had a chance to say as much to Chris, he saw the woman sitting on the porch steps waiting. And the big car at the curb didn't look like it belonged to the neighbors.

3 ....

Jock walked slowly across the lawn toward the stranger, Chris clinging uncertainly to his hand. He nodded to her. "Afternoon, ma'am."

The woman rose slowly and looked from him to the boy and back, her smile pleasant but unconvincing. "Good afternoon, I'm looking for a Mr. Ransome."

"I'm the only Mr. Ransome there is now. Reckon you was looking for my son Andy that got killed, though." He looked down at Chris. "This young'un's papa, he was."

"I know," she said, "and that's why I'm here. I'm Mrs. Worthington, with the children's division of the county assistance agency, and it's you I want to see." She glanced once more at the boy. "Privately."

Jock roughed his hand through Chris's hair, making light of it. "Reckon me and the boy got no secrets now."

"I don't mean to make secrets," she said, "but it would be better if we talked alone."

"About what?"

"About—conditions." Her embarrassment was becoming more and more obvious. "It shouldn't take too long."

Jock leaned down and gently rubbed his thigh where a cramp suddenly caught at the muscle. "Well, guess it can't hurt none. Boy, you run along in the kitchen, get you a cookie, and take it out in the yard. Tell you what—maybe you can drive them horseshoe stakes in the back ground, near the spindly oak, you know. And soon's the lady leaves, me and you can pitch a game." He straightened up. "Run along now."

Chris looked at him, clearly unwilling to go but just as certain that he must. "She said something about children, maybe she wants to talk about why I didn't go to school last week." He looked at the woman. "I didn't go because my mommy and daddy died." He swallowed after the words, but he could not suck them back.

"No," she said, "it's not school. And I know about your mother and father, and I'm dreadfully sorry."

Everybody said their sorries, Jock thought. He patted Chris on the shoulder. "See—it's not even you she means to talk about. Now run along like Paw-paw says," he said, "and I'll be there d'rectly."

When the boy had gone, Jock led the woman into the living room. He was starting to point to a chair when

Chris came running back. "Paw-paw. Paw-paw!" He grabbed Jock's arm. "They stole things, somebody came in and stole lots of things. They got the television and the washing machine, and I don't know what all." His voice came wild and broken.

Jock caught his shoulder, held it with the little firmness the day had left him. "Now hold on," he said, "hold your horses. Didn't nobody steal anything, Paw-paw sent'em all back. The t-and-v, the washing machine, the bed back yonder, and even the settee."

"How come you sent 'em back? How come? Mommy liked them all, specially the sofa."

"I know, I know," Jock said. "But they wasn't paid for, boy, and wasn't nobody to pay for 'em now."

"But mommy and daddy'd bought 'em," the boy insisted. "I know 'cause I was with them when they did. I saw 'em pay the money. Now I don't have a TV to watch."

"They didn't truly buy'em, boy. They gave something down and meant to pay by the month."

The boy looked squarely into his face then. "But they're dead now. And that store where they bought the things, they wouldn't take 'em back, even if they weren't paid for."

"It was a debt, boy, a debt your pa'd of paid off, but he couldn't. And we wouldn't want your pa in his grave with debts hanging over his head, now would we?"

Very slowly, the boy lowered his head and half turned away. "No, sir, I reckon not. But now I don't have a TV to look at, and just chairs to sit on." He turned, took one slow step, another, then scurried from the room.

"I'm sorry," the woman said. "If you want to go see about him, I'll wait."

Jock shook his head. "No'm, no need to. Rough on him, losin' his folks like he done, and not knowin' what has to be took care of. But he's a young kid, smart'un, too, he'll learn soon enough. Just have to tender him some." Again he pointed to the chair. "Now, what's it you want to see me about?"

She sat on the edge of the chair and leaned stiffly forward. "It's—you and the boy. One of your neighbors was kind and thoughtful enough to call us about your plight. I came to offer our help."

Jock scratched the side of his nose, then began massaging his left knee. "Don't reckon we got a plight. Got trouble, me and the boy, figuring out how to make it alone, his folks didn't leave nothin' and all. 'Course, we can't stay for long in this big house, just me and him. But I ain't past goin', and he's young. Guess we'll just make do."

"Mr. Ransome, that's precisely why I'm here. Legally, the boy's an orphan now, no mother and no father."

"He's got a grandpa. That's blood kin."

"If you don't mind telling me," the woman asked, "how old are you?"

"Never made a secret of my age yet. Was born in '95—Monday, February 11, 1895. Only snowy day we had all that winter, my pa told me."

"You look well and healthy, too, but Mr. Ransome,

there are child-welfare laws we must abide by. A seventy-two-year-old grandfather simply doesn't meet the criteria, no matter how well intended." She looked about the room. "Unless," she said, "there's money enough to hire help."

Jock felt a sort of tingling along his spine, and the hair at the nape of his neck began to itch. He swallowed hard and rubbed his chin as if he had a beard that needed smoothing down. "Makes sense to me. Kids got to have more than an old wore-out man to see to 'em. I know, I was a kid myself once and remember what a rascal I was. Run off to the country one day myself, and had both Ma and Pa, even a sister and two older brothers, looking out after me. No, ma'am, a kid can't get by, not having no more than one old man to see to him."

The woman's expression seemed to go soft all of a sudden, as if she had expected him to argue, and he had not. "Well, Mr. Ransome," she said, "I'm glad to find you so sensible. Through our agencies we have many ways of seeing to a young boy's wants and needs. There's one home down in Richmond, and one in Charlottesville, too. And we have numerous foster homes."

"Yes'm. Figure there's some in the D of C, too—ought to be, big as it is. A boy needs more than an old man's grumps to keep him goin'." He turned on the seat and began scratching the other knee. "But the thing is, with school almost out, 'pears a shame he can't stay on here for a spell. Coupla weeks."

"Oh? You'll be able to stay on here that long?"

"Yes'm. Banker said so this mornin' when I turned in the papers. Told me it'd take maybe a month or so to get the court papers in order. Seems courts can't never do nothin' right now."

"But can you get along? Can you cook and look after the house?" As she pressed him, the smile faded. "I don't mean to pry, Mr. Ransome, but can you do what has to be done? Even two weeks can be a long time."

"Been gettin' by for four days now; me an' the boy'll make do." He reached across with his right hand and rubbed away a little sharp pang, remembering but not saying so, that he had forgotten to eat at midday.

The woman misinterpreted the motion. "Mr. Ransome, do—do you have a bad heart?"

"Ticker's good as ever." Jock stopped rubbing.

"Well, that's fine." She started to get up. "Two weeks," she said. "Perhaps it would be best to complete the school year. I'll need some papers, anyway—the boy's name and age, information about his parents, birth certificate, court papers, too. Everything must be done properly, you know, in case somebody wants to give him a real home."

"Adopt him, you mean?"

She looked embarrassed. "At his age, Mr. Ransome, it's hard to find adoptive parents. But a foster home, we can probably work that out." She started toward the door. "Oh, yes, *you'll* want to go to a more suitable place, too. I'm sure you've thought about that."

"Been a trifle busy with the boy's business, but I'll chew on it, first chance I get."

"I don't mean to be interfering with your private life," she said, "but if we can be of any assistance, please let me know. There are several fine homes here in the county, and in the district there's an old soldier's home."

"Wasn't in the army." Jock got up, too, and saw her to the door. "But don't fret about me, I'll make out somehow; the boy's what counts first."

He watched her till she was down the porch steps and halfway across the lawn, then he turned back. "Chris," he called. A chair scraped softly across the floor in the next room. "Boy, come on out here."

The boy came slowly, biting his lower lip, arms folded across his chest, and fingers clutching at his crumpled shirt. His eyes were glazed over with tears getting ready to fall.

"You didn't go out in the yard like I told you," Jock said. "You was there all the time, listenin'." His own voice was husky. He sat down once more and pulled the boy closer to him. "Wasn't you?"

Chris nodded, stood there staring into the old man's face. Hurt was in his eyes and in the veins of his neck and at the corners of his mouth. "You're going to let her take me off someplace. I heard you. I heard you. I thought you were going to take care of me." The tears began to overflow. "How come you can't, Paw-paw?"

Jock caught the boy's narrow hips in the palms of his coarse hands, held to them, and felt the shivering underneath. "You heard me *listenin'*. You heard me lettin' her have her say. But you didn't hear me agree to nothin'. Did you now?"

"You said two weeks, till school's out, and you didn't tell her not to bring those papers. You didn't tell her not to come back."

Jock pulled him even closer and turned him till he was propped on his aching knee. "Boy, you remember long time ago, when you was just a little shaver, 'fore your folks brought you way up here to Virginny, me and you went fishin' down to the old crick, 'member that?"

Chris turned his head and studied the old man's face. "Yessir, I think so."

"And 'member the way I showed you to tautline fish, sit real still, keepin' the bait just off the bottom, and not jerkin' everytime something touched it?"

"I don't know if I do or not."

"Well, anyway," Jock said, "that's how we done it, me and you. You don't jerk at the line every nibble you get. Have to wait, make sure it's a big'un and he's got a good holt of it. So when you give it a jerk you hook 'im in the mouth."

"But that woman wasn't talking about fishing, and you weren't talking about fishing, either. It was me and where I was going to live and all. And you didn't tell her *no* about anything."

"Same as fishin'," Jock said, "fishin' for time. If I'd of come back at her, tellin' her to mind her own affairs an' we'd mind ours, no tellin' what she'd of done. Might of gone off to the sheriff an' come back with some of those legallike papers, sayin' what we got to do." He ran his weary hand through the boy's hair. "Paw-paw's had a busy day of it t'day, gettin' shed of your pa's debts. One thing we can't have is debts hangin' over him, an' him not bein' here to do nothing' about 'em, now can we?"

"Reckon not," the boy said.

"Paw-paw needs time to figure it all out for you an' me. Don't just yet know what we'll do; but one thing you can count on, boy, your Paw-paw ain't lettin' anybody take you away from me. Not now, an' not never." He patted the boy. "Now come on, we got time for some horseshoe pitchin', then Paw-paw's going to fix us a big potful of leftover chicken and p'tato stew."

They went out into the backyard and pitched three games. Jock won the first. He let Chris win the second. And by the time they got around to the third, his arms were tired and Chris won without any letting. It was almost dusk when they went into the kitchen. Chris brought his homework to the kitchen table and worked there while his grandfather used more utensils than he needed making a pot of hot stew. When it was ready, they said grace and then ate silently. Afterward, though there was still a little daylight left over because of the daylight-saving time, they bathed and went to bed.

In the room's vague-dusk dimness, Jock stared unseeing through the narrow slits of the venetian blinds. Truth was, he had not thought at all beyond this day, beyond taking care of the business matters that Andy had left untended. If he had given it a moment of his thinking, however, he would have realized how few days there were between now and the end of school, and how little time he had in which to arrive at a plan for their joint survival. For it would be a joint one, that he knew. No matter how well intentioned that Mrs. Worthington woman was—she meant well, he supposed, but never mind that, and never mind what the laws might or might not say about who was too old and who wasn't—the boy was his boy's son, and blood kin was blood kin, and nobody needn't think for a minute he'd turn his back on his own.

Trouble was, right now he didn't know which way he *could* turn.

Jock closed his eyes and shut away all the outside world. Perhaps it was the tiredness, or maybe it was what had to be done, he did not know, but the tightness within him broke. And he wept. He wept for the boy asleep in the other room, and he wept for the son who died, and for the son's wife who had no one else to weep for her, and he wept for the time that had been but was now no more. But, most of all, he wept for his own years and the precious time that he did not have.

4 ....

The next morning Jock walked Chris to school, and for a short while he stood at the corner across the street from the sprawling one-story building, watching as the guards controlled the uneven traffic, as the children scurried cheerfully from curb to curb, as mother-driven cars and station wagons filed to the curved entrance to discharge their noisy passengers. He watched, too, as Chris ambled slowly along a worn path to the wide steps and sat there and stared at the others without joining them. "Time," Jock said aloud, without meaning to, "it'll take the boy time."

The corner guard looked about. "I didn't understand you," she said.

"I wasn't talkin' to you, ma'am," Jock said.

He turned about and started off in another direction, toward the grocery store four blocks away. There he bought a half-pound slice of ham, a quarter of a pound of ground meat, a bunch of carrots, and five pounds of potatoes. He took the money from a battered black coin purse and rammed it back into his pants pocket.

"If you'd like, I'll have one of the boys put the sack in your car," the lady clerk said.

"Got no car," Jock said. "Nothin' to carryin' this, anyhow."

It took him almost thirty minutes to walk back to the house, and he was short of breath when he got there. He put the meat in the refrigerator and the potatoes and carrots in the cabinet under the sink. Then he spent no more than five minutes washing the breakfast dishes.

When that was done, he walked into the living room and dragged the old rocking chair through the front door and onto the porch. He took off his coat and hooked it over the chair's back so that the sleeves and pockets hung down on either side. Then he sat down and leaned back and closed his eyes and slowly rocked.

He sat there rocking and thinking all morning and into midafternoon—stopping once, only long enough to go inside for a boiled egg he'd fixed while he cooked breakfast and for a slice of bread and a cup of cold coffee. Except for that short break, he rocked and thought till his sense of sun and shadow measurement told him it was time to go get the boy.

When they returned home, Jock did not go back to the

chair. Once more, he and Chris whiled away the afternoon, pitching horseshoes. Once Chris asked, "Pawpaw, when's that lady coming back?"

Jock said, "Reckon she won't come back till next week."

The boy said, "You're going to tell her I'm staying with you, aren't you?"

Jock said back, "We'll see what's best to tell her."

"But you are going to tell her I'm staying with you, aren't you?"

"Boy, I told you I ain't leavin' you to no strangers. You're stayin' with me so stop your frettin'."

"You mean it?" the boy said. "You *really* mean it?"

"I really mean it."

That night he took the ham slice and fried it in the skillet. While it was cooking he opened a can of spinach and one of peaches. And when the meat was done, he halfway fried four slices of bread in the ham grease. They had that and diluted coffee for supper.

The next day Jock followed the same ritual except that he did not return to the grocery store. But he rocked and thought. That morning, though, he was interrupted once by the telephone. He started not to answer it, then remembered that there still might be business matters of Andy's that needed his seeing to. It was that woman, Mrs. Worthington. "Mr. Ransome, we need a little information for the official papers. How old were your son and his wife, and what were their full names, and how old is the boy? We'll need his full name, too."

Jock gave her the names and made up birth dates because he couldn't recall them offhand. "And you can put down that the boy's doin' tolerable well in school."

"Fine." Then she added, "Oh, by the way, Mr. Ransome, I had a chat with a Salvation Army representative about your case, a Major Hester. He suggested you call him; he may have some ideas for you. They have an excellent men's home, you know."

"That was right kind of you, ma'am." Jock hung up the phone properly to break the connection. Then he picked it up once more, and this time he slammed it onto its cradle.

An hour and a half later there was another interruption. This time it was the mailman walking across the lawns of the subdivision, whistling "Red River Valley" off-key.

"Morning." He handed Jock three envelopes, about bill size.

"Good day to you," Jock said.

"I'd like to swap places with you for the day," the man said, "rocking there like you had it made. Nice thing, not having anything to worry about, just sit and rock."

" 'Pears that way," Jock said. He drew hard on his pipe and said nothing more, and the mail carrier went on his way.

That afternoon was much like the one before. He went to the school corner for Chris, then spent the afternoon doing things with him. Difference was, they didn't pitch horseshoes. Chris dug out his baseball glove and the old one his father'd had, and they played a kind of catch. Jock had never worn a glove, and it felt awkward on his hand. And though he'd thrown rocks a few times in his manhood, he hadn't touched a ball since he married almost fifty years ago. But he tried. Once when he squatted to catch a low one, he fell and sat hard on the remnants of a compost pile that Stella'd had Andy fix for her. Chris laughed. It was the first time in more than a week that he'd so much as smiled.

For supper that evening, Jock fried two ground-meat patties and boiled the potatoes and carrots together. And once again, they drank diluted coffee, this time with ice and a little sugar in it.

Thursday started the same way. But shortly after ten o'clock that morning, Jock reached his decision. He got up from the rocker, tugged it to the door, and carried it back inside to its rightful place in the living room.

He put on his hat and coat and walked off in the other direction from the school toward a filling station he thought he remembered. He got a courtesy map of the southeastern states and went back home with it. He spread it out on the little dining table at the end of the living room—looked like the table never had been used, it was so clean and shiny. Then he turned on the basement lights and went down the narrow flight of stairs.

Andy had said that one day he meant to have his own workshop down there, but so far all he'd acquired was what was piled on the plywood workbench—a handsaw, two hammers, four different kinds of pliers, a small wrench, an old belly-bruising brace and bit, and a whole boxful of screwdrivers. Three wooden crates lined against the wall were neatly labeled Parts, but all three were empty except for half a dozen one-by-two strips Stella must have meant to use as tomato-plant stakes. On a shelf above the table were seven jars, each containing nails or screws.

Jock looked carefully at everything he saw, relating the items to the needs he had decided upon. The wood was there, all he had to do was tear up two of the crates; the screws which he preferred to nails were in the jars, and the hand tools would be enough. He went back upstairs and rummaged through the closets till he found the yardstick he had seen Stella use. Then he returned to the basement and stuck the pipe in the corner of his mouth and went to work.

When his hands were tired and his shoulders ached from the sawing, he stood back and surveyed the results. Half the pieces he needed were cut, and there was enough wood for the rest; but the fitting and joining and putting together would take longer than he'd imagined. It would have to be solid and sturdy enough to hold together for a long journey. Wouldn't do to have it come apart on the way, for he couldn't carry all the tools along. Good thing, he guessed, that he had the rest of this week and all of the next to finish it.

He went back upstairs and made himself a cheese sandwich and poured a glass of water. He sat at the table where the map was and studied the crazy pattern of black and green and red lines extending up and down and across it. He put one finger on Washington, D.C., and another on Birmingham, Alabama, because they were the closest cities to where he was and where he meant to go, and he glanced back and forth along the intervening geography. A terrible long way to go, he said to himself, a terrible long way.

When he finished eating, he folded the map and put it away. Not time to tell the boy about it, not yet, getting through the rest of this week and all of next would be enough for him to fret about. Besides, he might slip and say something to one of his classmates or maybe to the teacher, and word might somehow get back to that Worthington woman. He couldn't chance that.

He washed his hands very carefully and he looked to make certain he had no traces of sawdust on his pants or shirt before he left the house and went after Chris.

All day long Friday, while Chris was in school, Jock worked in the basement. He didn't go downstairs once during the weekend, didn't let on that he was doing anything special about his promise to Chris. But Monday and Tuesday and Wednesday he did the same. He cut and sawed and measured and set screws till his fingers hurt and his wrists ached. Midmorning on Wednesday, he had it all done except the wheels. He had already spotted those—on an old wagon that Chris no longer played with. Putting them on his creation took a little doing—he couldn't use the regular kind of brackets because he wanted to be able to remove them. He solved the problem by cutting a shallow notch in the bottom and used turning wooden catches like those on some of the old barn doors to hold the axle in place.

Finally, he took the old wagon tongue and attached it with a long bolt and wing nut from one of the jars. He found a can of lavender paint Stella had intended using on a flower box outside the kitchen window, and he gave the whole thing, except for the white wagon wheels, one thick coat.

Done, he stood back and looked at it. It would do. Time now to make the boy part of the plan.

That afternoon while they were walking home from school, Chris said, "Paw-paw, remember that woman who talked to you about me?"

"Yep."

"Well, she came to school today. Talked to my teacher."

"Did, huh?"

"She looked at me and the teacher looked at me."

"Reckon you looked back at 'em," Jock said.

"I looked, but not either one said anything to me. I wonder how come."

"Maybe she wanted to see you was at school like I said."

"I thought for a moment she was going to take me out of the room." Chris kicked at a pebble.

The idea brought a frown to Jock's mind but he did not let it show on his face. "Boy, ain't but two more days till school's done for the year. She'd of tried doin' it last week if that's what she had a mind to do."

"But maybe she'll come back tomorrow, or maybe Friday," Chris said.

"S'posin' she does," Jock said. "Just tell 'er to come

see me 'fore she does anything else. But don't tell 'er we got plans, me an' you."

Chris seemed to think about that for a few minutes. He walked on ahead and kicked another rock off the sidewalk. Then he waited for Jock to catch up with him. "When are you going to tell me?"

"Today'll do. Soon's we get to the house I'll tell you."

But when they reached the house, a car was parked at the curb and a man was sitting at the wheel. As Jock and Chris started across the lawn, the man got out and came around the side. "Mr. Ransome?"

Jock stopped and looked at him. He had on a uniform that was unlike a policeman's. Perhaps it was the uniform that prompted Chris to clutch Jock's hand. "That's me," Jock said.

"I'm Major Hester from the Salvation Army." He glanced at Chris and the trace of a smile was gentle. "I had a long talk with Mrs. Worthington the other day. She said you might like to see me."

"Mighty thoughtful of her," Jock said. "Been meanin' to call, but there's so much to do."

"I understand," the man said. Simple politeness dictated that Jock ask the man to come inside, and he had to force himself not to do so.

"You know the boy's welfare comes first," the man said.

Jock felt Chris's hand press tighter. "Reckon it does, old folks like me ain't pushed to do anything in a hurry. What time we got left, we take it easy. Lady said you got places for folks like me to stay. Reckon you got work for 'em, too."

"Those that can work," the man said, "we have odd jobs for. Those that for one reason or another can't, aren't expected to."

"I've heard tell of your good works," Jock said. "Never figured to lean on you, though."

"You can lean on us, Mr. Ransome." Major Hester smiled again. He stood nearby, uncertainly now, as if he had expected an invitation inside and when it did not come he was not sure whether to stand or go.

"Trouble is," Jock went on, "I never cottoned to charity."

"But we don't look upon our homes as charity," the man said. "It's a service, the kind of thing you'd do for me if our positions were reversed."

Jock squinted his eyes and stared hard at Major Hester. "Maybe you don't at that, and maybe if I was in your shoes and you was in mine I'd give you the offer of help. Mister, let me do for the boy, then we'll see about me."

The man reached inside his shirt pocket and pulled forth a small white card. He handed it to Jock. "My phone number," he said. "Give me a call when you're ready to talk. I think there's a way of helping the body without hurting the dignity."

Jock took the card and read off the number aloud. "I thank you, mister."

After he'd driven away, Chris looked up at Jock. "That's not what you promised. You promised wasn't anybody going to take me from you or you from me."

"Boy," Jock said, "I didn't tell him anything. You think on what I said. I told him nothing."

"But he gave you the card," Chris said.

"And I thanked him," Jock said. "You thank folks when they offer help, even if you don't aim to take it." He ran his hand through Chris's hair and guided him toward the porch. "Now, let's see to our business."

Inside the house, he led the way to the basement steps and turned on the light. "Come on, let's go see what I made."

It was there in the middle of the floor just as he'd left it, the freshly painted surface glistening in the light of the unshaded drop-cord bulb. The boy walked up to it and stared. He backed off and moved around it and stopped on the other side and stared again. "Neat," he said, "it's neat." His voice for once was quick-edged and light. "What is it?"

"It's the gitaway box," Jock said, "for totin' our plunder on the trip you an' me're takin' come Saturday."

Chris kept staring at the creation. "I didn't know we were going on a trip. Nobody said anything about a trip."

"Paw-paw don't always say what he's thinkin' till he's thought it out good," Jock told him. "We're goin' down yonder, me an' you, back home."

The boy's eyes got wide and now he looked at his grandfather. "All the way down to Alabama," he whispered, "to where we used to live? I guess we're going on a train or maybe an airplane. I never have been on a train," he added.

"Nope, got no money for trains or airyplanes."

"Well I guess a bus'll take us that far." Chris sounded doubtful.

"No bus, neither," Jock said, "leastwise not far." He sniffed hard. "Boy, it takes money for them things, an' Paw-paw ain't got much. Time we pay the bills your pa didn't get to, wouldn't have enough for one of us to ride, let alone two."

He came closer and surveyed the object. "Like it, boy? Here, let me show you how it works." Carefully, he unhooked a latch on the side and let it down, making sure nothing touched the fresh paint. Inside it, smoothly finished partitions divided the space into seven cache sections. He pointed them out one by one. "This big'un's for a blanket, a kind of a sleepin' bag I made out of a old quilt your ma had, and this'un's for some clothes—we'll need a change o' underwear an' socks, an' maybe a shirt. And this'un's for cookin' an' eatin' tools, a little skillet and a pot an' a coupla them plastic cups. This'un over here in the corner's for vittles, like canned goods an' prunes an' dried apples, an' maybe a box of that powdery milk. Seen a box in one of them kitchen cabinets." He pointed to a smaller one near the top. "This here's for soap an' a washrag an' a towel an' your toothbrush—you been brushin' your teeth regular, ain't you?"

"Yes, sir."

"An' this one right here in the middle's for tools we might need." He stopped then, letting the boy study the shelves.

"What's that one for?" He pointed to the smallest.

Jock took a deep breath and touched Chris's shoulder. "Boy, there's a old cigar box your pa kept special meanin' things in. Figured you'd want to take that along, an' maybe a picture or two of your ma an' pa, can't carry much extra." Before Chris could let his thoughts drift to something else, Jock pointed to the squarish area in the middle. "This'un's for what I like best."

"You didn't tell me about that one," the boy said.

"It's for fishin' lines an' corks an' hooks, an' a slingshot in case we come across a rabbit or a squirrel, or maybe even a wild turkey."

Slowly, unbelievingly, the boy turned toward Jock. "If we're not going to ride on a train or even a bus, are we going to *walk* all the way? And camp out?"

"Ain't no other way, as I see it," Jock said. "Figure to ride a bus the first hunnert mile, get away from folks like that Worthington woman an' that fella Major Hester or whatever. 'Course, he wasn't such a bad fella, seemed pretty nice, an' that Salvation Army I've heard tell is a fine outfit. But Paw-paw don't know about laws an' things, an' there may be some law says if a boy your age ain't got anybody 'cept an old man of blood kin to see to him, one of them welfare agencies has got to do it. Might even have the sheriff or a po-lice come make us do what we don't mean to. So we'll spend a little money to get out of here fast, then we'll make it on our own from there."

"But that's a long way. When we left there and came up here, Daddy drove for two whole days. No telling how many days it'll take us, just walking."

"Boy, if you look at the far end of anything you got to do, it's a long way off. Like pickin' cotton or goin' to school. You get to thinkin' about pickin' while you're plowin', an' August seems like a long way off. An' next summer seems a-way in the future on the first day back to school, don't it?" He stopped and Chris nodded slowly. "Now look at the map of where we are an' how far it is to Bucksville, an' it looks like you couldn't never get there walkin'. But by cracky we'll make it. You know something, my pa walked clean to Texas an' back when he was a young man, I mean, across the Mississippi River an' past N'Orlean an' all the way to San Antone. An' he made it. Some said he was a bigger man when he got back than when he left out."

The boy turned and walked to the stairway and sat huddled on the bottom step. "That was a long time ago," he said, "before they had busses and cars. Folks had to walk."

"Could of rid a horse if he'd had one," Jock said, "but he didn't, he was that pore." He walked over and hunched down beside Chris, put his hand on the boy's knee. "Just looky at the fun me an' you'll have, sleepin' out in the open, listenin' to the night sounds—you know, birds goin' to sleep an' crickets an' maybe a old bullfrog. You ever hear a bullfrog croakin' at night, boy? Sounds like he done swallered a drum an' don't know how to spit it out."

"I heard one a long time ago," Chris said, "but I didn't like it." He chewed on his finger. "Paw-paw, maybe somebody'd give us the money to ride the train, maybe that man at the bank you saw. Or that man who was here a while ago. Said he'd help, maybe he'd give us money for a train or bus ticket."

Jock sat down beside the boy and sighed heavily. "Gimme," he said, "gimme-gimme. Trouble with the world today, boy, is the gimmies, everybody's got 'em. Years back, folks'd come around to the door askin' for whatever you could give 'em, an' other folks called 'em beggars. 'Course some'd feel sorry for 'em an' maybe give 'em wore-out clothes or moldy bread an' table scraps. An' them fellas was always lookin' at the ground; done got so beholden to everybody they couldn't look up. Even countries is that way now. I ain't smart, but I been readin' the newspapers, an' there's always some country or another comin' over to that Washington D of C askin' for a handout. They can't look up, neither.

"No, sir, boy, we'll work an' walk it, you an' me. An' you wait—see if you don't have a time of it, get to see a lot more o' the country than you ever could look at from a train or bus window. Reckon you'll learn things, too."

"But that's why I go to school," the boy said, "to learn."

"You'll be learnin' things ain't ever been inside a school book. Time you get to Bucksville, no tellin' how much you'll be able to tell them new teachers."

Chris leaned over and fidgeted with his shoestring. He got up and walked over to the lavender creation Jock had spend so much time on, ran his finger over the still sticky surface. "Mommy meant to have a flower box this color." He looked at Jock. "What about them?"

"What about 'em?"

"Don't know how they'd like for us to go off and leave them."

"Boy, the best of your ma an' pa is in your heart. An' never mind, they'd think a heap of you, workin' to get where your pa's sister is, 'stead of lettin' some gov'ment office put you in a orphan's home."

Chris turned back toward him, and there was something new and different in his eyes. "You think so? Do you really think so?"

"I *know* it, boy! Your pa done some bad things when he was a young'un, got into some terrible scrapes, nobody need tell me what he done. He come out of it, though, with the help of that good woman he married. Reckon he was a lot of things, but one thing he wasn't. He wasn't a deadbeat, an' he wouldn't want his son to be one, neither. What he done good, he done hisself, scrappin' all the way an' askin' no quarter of nobody. He could look straight up to the sky if he was of a mind."

The boy leaned over and stared hard at one of the box's inner partitions. Then very deliberately he straightened up to his full height and turned and faced his grandfather. "All right, I'll walk fast as I can and work, too, if I've got to, as long as you don't go off and leave me."

"Boy, I ain't about to leave you," Jock said.

5 ....

Another five or six minutes and the bus would be in Charlottesville, the end of the line for him and the boy. Jock shifted slightly and let his hand dangle down till the fingers touched the smooth surface of the gitaway box, half blocking the aisle. It wasn't that he cared about it getting scratched, and its contents were carefully stowed so nothing would rattle or spill if it were turned on its side. But he'd objected to putting it in the storage compartment because he didn't want to go to the terminal. According to his map, the route the bus took and the one he wanted out of the city crossed, and that's where he meant to get off.

He glanced casually at Chris, sitting near the window

and leaning forward so he could see out. The boy was doing fine, hadn't said much and hadn't even asked for water except that once, back at the town called Culpeper or some such. He'd said nothing at all about their leaving. Not a word.

Their departure had been quick and simple. After eating three pieces of buttered toast and drinking the last of the milk, they had simply walked out of the house and closed the door behind them. Jock had locked it, then put the key in an envelope along with a note he had written to Mr. Timothy Braddock at the bank. He had dropped that in a mailbox they passed on their way to the little shopping center where they'd boarded the bus, confident that, just as he'd planned it, on a Saturday like this the letter wouldn't go to anybody till Monday and not till then would anyone know he and the boy were gone. He also mailed a terse postcard to Jessica, saying they were on their way and would be there when they got there.

True, Chris had stopped at the corner farthest from the house and started to look back, but Jock had caught his shoulder gently. "Boy," he had said, "it's what's ahead you got to look to. Behind you is gone." The boy had hesitated for a brief moment, then he'd clutched hard at the gitaway box's hauling tongue and started down the sidewalk.

"Paw-paw, when'll we be to where we're getting off?"

Jock listened to the traffic sounds that came muffled through the bus window. "In a minute or so. Reckon you're tired of sittin'."

"A little," the boy said, "but I wish we could keep riding."

"Maybe we'll get to ride some more down the road a-piece."

The bus stopped at a traffic light, and the driver looked half around. "Mister, you wanted to know when we get to the route 250 intersection."

"If that's the way to someplace called Waynesboro, that's what I want," Jock said.

"Be the next corner," the driver said.

Jock nudged Chris. "You hear that, boy?" he said.

"Gettin' off soon now. Paw-paw'll sure be glad to stretch his legs some."

Chris settled back briefly. "Guess mine'll be stretched walking. We're going to start walking now, aren't we?"

"Yep," Jock said, "reckon so."

When the bus stopped to let them off, Jock made his way slowly forward, the gitaway box bumping seat arms and passenger arms alike. "'Scuse me, 'scuse me. Terrible sorry, ma'am."

"Oughtn't let things like that be put on a bus," a woman muttered.

"No'm, reckon not," Jock said. "If I was you I'd speak to the driver about it." With his free hand he tipped his hat to her and almost bumped another passenger in the face with his elbow.

"C'me on, mister. I don't have all day," the driver said.

Jock puffed through the door and down the two short

steps to the ground, taking care not to let the corner of the box get caught on the rail. He looked at the driver and nodded to him. "Thank you, mister. You sure know how to handle that contraption."

The door shut and the bus moved away with the traffic.

Jock lugged the box from the curb and onto a service station's access apron. He took his time opening the side and taking out the wheels and tongue. "Here, boy," he said, "might as well learn now as later. Set the wheel axle in place while I hold it up for you." It took Chris over five minutes to work it into the slot firmly and turn the little latches that held it in place. It took almost that much longer to fit the tongue onto its bracket and fix the bolt and wing nut.

One of the service station attendants walked over, hand on hip. "Pop, how about taking your business someplace else; you're blockin' my drive."

Jock studied the man from his heavy lace-up broggans to the smear of grease across his forehead. "Pretty prosperous place you got here," he said. "Must do a heap of business. Reckon you couldn't use any help, though."

"No help wanted," the man said. "Don't guess you'd know a sparkplug from a carburetor, anyhow."

"I'd know dirt," Jock said, "an' seems from your 'pearance you could use some cleanin' up around here."

Chris touched his arm. "I got it done, Paw-paw."

"Never mind the cracks," the service station man said, "just get that buggy out of the way."

Jock touched Chris's shoulder with his elbow. "Let's go, boy," he said.

They crossed the street and turned left in the direction that the arrow and road sign saying route 250 pointed.

Chris tugged away at the box. Jock helped him wiggle-waggle around three people coming abreast down the sidewalk, ignoring the way one of them paused and stared at the lavender box. After five blocks the sidewalk ran out, and they worked their way onto the dirt shoulder of the street that had now become the highway. Chris stopped once to shift and pull with his left hand. "Paw-paw, how long'll it take us to get to Bucksville?"

Jock studied a while. "Some time," he said.

"Seven or eight days?

"More like five or six weeks. But never mind. We ain't in a hurry; ain't nobody waitin' on us."

"Reckon we'll *really* get there?"

"We'll get there."

Two hours later they reached a rise in the road and could see a freshly painted billboard. Jock looked at it. "Mont-kella," he muttered. "Wonder what that is."

Chris looked at the word more carefully. "Not Mont-kella, it's Monticello."

"Some kind of park, I guess," Jock said.

"Not a park, it's a house. Teacher said if we ever got down here we ought to see it."

"See a house?"

"It's not just any house," Chris said. "It's where

Thomas Jefferson lived a long time ago."

"Well," Jock said, "never figured to run up on it. He was president near two hunnert years ago, wasn't he?"

"My history book says he was the third president of the United States."

"House must be in pretty bad shape by now," Jock said.

"No, sir," Chris said, "some people have been keeping it up for him." He paused at the driveway and looked down it. "It's what they call a shrine, I think that's what teacher said." He looked at his grandfather. "Sure would like to see where a president lived."

Jock stared at the carefully kept shrubbery marking the entrance. "Well, s'pose we go take a look at it. Ain't in a hurry to get nowhere."

It took another ten minutes to work their way along the edge of the drive to a wide walk leading toward even wider steps and a columned porch. Jock stared at the red brick mansion. "Looks to be in might good repair. You right sure of what you're sayin', 'bout it bein' that old?"

"That's what teacher said."

They pulled the gitaway box up on the sidewalk and over to the side of the steps. Jock opened the box and took out a length of rope he had stuffed in beside the blanket. He tied one end to the handle and hooked the other around one of the huge columns. Not till he'd tied it did he notice the woman sitting at a small table to the side of the heavy glass doors, staring disapprovingly.

"Sir, couldn't you have left that in your car?"

"Got no car," Jock said, "but I reckon it'll be safe

there till we get out if you'd be so kind as to keep an eye on it." He and Chris went up the steps and started inside.

"One minute, sir, that'll be $1.60."

Jock stared at her, admiring the high cut of her blouse, the long sleeves, and the skirt that came down over her legs so that it flounced out about her chair. "Ma'am, we ain't aimin' to buy nothin'. Just want to take a look, the boy's teacher said he ought to see it."

"I know, sir," she said. "The $1.60 is the admission price, a dollar for you and sixty cents for the boy."

Jock scratched the side of his neck. "Mean to tell me it costs that much just to look?"

"I'm sorry, sir, but it does."

Jock looked down at Chris. "Boy, best we can do is walk around an' see the outside, can't squander a buck-sixty just to look."

Chris peeped around the half-open door and stared toward the inside. He backed away a step, then another, still looking. "Sure would like to see that table over yonder close up," he said.

Jock caught his shoulder lightly. "Maybe someday you can come back. Time you get growed up, maybe you'll have the price of lookin'." He glanced at the woman. "Thank you anyway, ma'am, an' if I ain't speakin' out of turn, you're dressed mighty nice, good to see a woman covered proper."

"It's our way of being dressed as the women were in Mr. Jefferson's day," she said.

"Well, you keep it up," Jock said. "The way young

womenfolks dress today, seems like it won't be long 'fore they won't be wearin' nothin' but hairnets an' belly belts." He tugged at Chris's shoulder. "Let's go, boy, we'll circle 'er once, then take to the road again."

They were halfway down the steps when the woman called out, "Sir."

Jock looked about. "Yes, ma'am."

She didn't seem quite certain how to say it. "Sir, we have a special charge for school boys and girls; of course, school's out, but since his teacher said he ought to see Monticello—it'd be just half a dollar for him."

Jock hesitated and took a deep breath and sighed it out. "Ma'am, that's mighty kind, but me an' the boy can't even spare that much today."

He untied the rope and they started slowly back up the sidewalk. They were at the end of it, just passing a carefully laidout corner garden of boxwoods, when Jock stopped and peered hard at the shrubbery. "Boy, you wait up a minute." He handed Chris the wagon tongue and returned to the wide porch. "Ma'am, that patch of bushes yonder, there's a bunch of wild onions and crab grass 'bout to take it over. Reckon it'd be worth the price of the boy goin' in for me to weed it?"

The woman hesitated. "Well, sir, it's unusual." Then she smiled. "But we don't like weeds here. Send him along and we'll put him with the next group."

Jock took his pocketknife and opened the large blade. He dug with it and with his fingers till the black mulch was cleared of every wild onion sprout and crab grass shoot. He was just finishing when Chris came out after his tour. “Did you like it, boy?” Jock said over his shoulder.

“Yes, sir, you just ought to see some of his inventions. Nobody ever said anything about his inventions in school.”

“You tell me about it while we walk,” Jock said.

He got up finally and brushed off the knees of his trousers and went back to the porch and thanked the woman for letting Chris in. He rejoined his grandson and caught the wagon handle. “My time to pull,” he said. “But we made a mistake this mornin’. We come east from that town ’stead of goin’ west, got to backtrack to that Charlottesville place an’ go toward the mountains.”

“I thought we took the right number road,” the boy said.

“Did,” Jock said, “but it goes both ways.”

“You mean we lost all that time?”

Jock shook his head. “Don’t figure it’s losin’ time when you learn somethin’; anyhow, goin’ fast don’t always get you where you want to go. Look about you an’ see things, let it mellow inside you for a spell—you get smarter a heap quicker that way. Don’t you fret, we’ll get to Bucksville, you an’ me.”

6 ....

Jock's legs ached with the kind of bone-dead tiredness that he used to feel after the first full day of spring plowing, muscles aquiver, his feet pressure-tender.

For five hours they had walked westward, retracing their path to Charlottesville and away again, this time in the right direction. For a while, Chris had pulled the gitaway box alone, but he was less accustomed to walking than his grandfather, Jock discovered; and if the old one had not urged them on the young one would have lingered back at that wide open place where a railroad track crossed the highway or at the junction where one road turned north and the route they wanted to follow continued toward the mountain. A mile out of the city,

Jock had taken the handle and, except for one short haul going downhill from the train crossing, he had done all the pulling.

Now Jock felt that he could pull no more; but as he watched his grandson struggling to keep up, he clamped down hard on the words that would have owned up to his own weariness. "Boy, the road sign back a-ways said there was an overlook point just ahead; maybe that's a pullin'-off place."

"You mean a place to stop?"

"Maybe so," Jock said.

The boy forced himself to walk straight, stretching to look beyond a gradual curve. "Sure hope so. I'm tired, Paw-paw."

"Reckon it's the most walkin' you ever done," Jock said.

"I never had to walk much since we came up here," the boy said. "Sure must be a long way to Bucksville."

"Long enough."

Beyond the bend, the roadside park turned out to be a shallow gravel drive off to the left, with a battered picnic table and two benches, a barrel-shaped trash container, and what looked to be a water hydrant sticking up out of the ground and supported by a concrete post. A narrow rock wall guarded the overlook from the wilderness of thick tree growth below. "Yonder it is," Jock said, "an' looks like they got water."

"Sure be glad to have some." Chris brightened.

"Don't drink too much right off," Jock said, "wet your gullet first."

He let the boy go ahead, then he took his turn, filling his mouth and sloshing the cool liquid against his cheeks and over his tongue before spitting it out, then taking another and swallowing it. He sat on one of the benches and looked out over the trees. "Won't be long 'fore dark; reckon we might as well make camp here t'night."

"Right up here beside the road?"

"Nope," Jock said, "down yonder out o' sight, behind one o' them clumps. You spot us one."

Chris walked to the retaining wall and leaned over it. "I see one, not far down and there's a path going to it."

They weren't the first to use the spot. A weather-beaten carton of empty beer bottles rested against the trunk of a tree, and a tattered old hat was caught in a blackberry bush. A piece of paper with its writing long since faded was impaled in the bush's thorns. "It'll do," Jock said. He got down on his knees beside the gitaway box and unfastened the side. "Git me some dry twigs, but leave off the grass, don't want nothin'll cause smoke."

Chris looked, but in the end Jock had to find his own twigs. Once he had them, it took only a few minutes to get a small fire going. He opened the one can of hash he'd found in Stella's cabinet and dumped its contents in the small boiler. "Shame to get such a shiny pan all smutted up," he said. He held it over the open flame till it began to sizzle.

Chris sat down and leaned against the box.

"Sure gets hungry walking."

"This'll fill up the hollows," Jock said. "You get them

pie tins out, and there's a box of crackers, get them, too."

"What're we going to drink?" Chris asked.

"Reckon you can go take them cups an' bring us some water."

"Just water?"

"I brung the last of the cocoa powder stuff," Jock said. "You want that, we'll stir you some."

They ate silently, Jock washing down the thick hash and dry crackers with short swallows, Chris relishing the taste of the chocolate as he made it override the chopped potato bits and occasional slivers of stringy meat. When they'd finished, Jock said, "Now you take this here pan an' go wash it out; bring it back full." While he was gone, Jock fingered inside the box where only the blanket was supposed to be stored. He located the little package of cookies he had hidden away, and when Chris came back, he handed it to the boy. "Figure a growin' young'un ought to eat more'n an old man. Grab yourself two or three."

"Didn't know you had them."

"Makes 'em taste better when you don't know about 'em," Jock said.

He boiled out the pan and the cups and pie tins and put them in the compartment of the gitaway box where they belonged. And just before the last shadows of the evening disappeared he took the blanket and spread it over the smoothest spot of ground he could find. He had sewn it together with heavy thread, double stitched it, and tied heavy knots in it at all the corners. It was made so the seam ran up the middle, and two corner flaps folded back. "You take that side, an' Paw-paw'll take this'un." He slipped off his trousers and rolled them and his coat into a kind of pillow, placing the bundle beneath the blanket to keep it smooth. Together, then, they slipped into the makeshift sleeping bag.

Up on the road, the occasional car going downhill and the trucks going uphill roared away the silence. Chris muttered something about them once, then half turned toward Jock. "Paw-paw, when other boys' and girls' mothers and daddies die, do they run off, too?"

"Some go to state farms, some go to those orphans' homes, some go to their kin, an' I reckon some do run."

"When some folks die, it sure does make things different for other folks," the boy said.

"Does, indeed. Now you sleep, you hear. Good night, boy."

Jock took a deep breath, held it a moment, then exhaled slowly. He did it a second time and a third, and he knew the pain was more than weariness, the quick, sharp stab was more than a muscle objecting to this kind of effort. The little tablet he had slipped beneath his tongue while the boy went after water had left a bitterness in his mouth, a dryness in his throat. He had thought to rest when he went to Andy's, hadn't meant to take this kind of journey. Like the boy said, when a body dies, it sure makes it different for another body. He closed his eyes to the darkness and his ears to the sounds above. Outside the blanket, his hard fingers found the boy's softer ones, and he slept.

It was daylight when the slamming of a car door awakened them. Quickly Chris slipped out of the blanket and into his shoes. Jock moved less swiftly, taking time to work his legs into his trousers before standing. "Boy," he said, "there's four eggs in the box, a dab of grease, coupla slices of bread. You run up an' get some water while I get a fire goin'. Hot coffee'll start the day right."

The boy had been gone only half a minute and Jock was busy scaring up twigs for the fire when the wooded silence was sliced wide open at the seams by a woman's scream. Jock stopped and turned just as Chris came flailing through the underbrush. "There's a woman up there!" His lips worked and his arm pointed back through the trees. "She was standing there, looking off at the mountains. I guess she didn't hear me coming. When she saw me, she sure hollered."

Jock caught him, held him close. "Musta been her slammin' that car door up to the pull-off."

The boy was trembling against him. "Scared me. I didn't know anybody was up there."

"Reckon it startled her some, too," Jock said.

"You don't think she'll come looking for me, do you?" the boy asked. "Maybe I ought to go tell her excuse me."

"No," Jock said, "ain't no point in sayin' nothin' to her."

Once again a car door slammed, followed by the grind and the roar as a car engine came to life. Tires skidded on loose gravel, squealed as they made contact with the hard road's surface. "Done gone, anyhow," Jock said.

He stood there for a moment, letting the boy settle down. He couldn't be sure now, maybe she was gone and wouldn't come back, or maybe she would go looking for one of those highway patrolmen, the kind that drove those gray cars with the blue stripes down the sides and the big red light on top. Maybe one of them would come looking to see what a young boy like Chris was doing here alone, and maybe he would arrest them for camping out.

Jock picked up the blanket and took his time folding it and putting it back in the gitaway box. He took the pan from Chris and put it in the proper cubicle, made certain that everything was in the right place, and closed the side.

It wasn't just a policeman in the woods that worried him, not even if they were doing wrong by building a fire and camping at the roadside. It was that back-up-yonder business about the law and orphans that he wasn't sure about. Perhaps that woman had not told him everything; could be that with both his folks dead, Chris didn't belong to him now; could be he belonged to the state. Wasn't right taking blood kin away and putting him in a home or giving him to somebody else, but you couldn't be certain.

Jock decided not to share that worry with the boy.

"Reckon we ought to go on," he said.

"Without breakfast?" the boy said.

Jock handed him one of the two slices of bread he had held out. "Here, you chew on that an' I'll chew on the other'n. We'll drink us some water up there at the faucet."

"How come we can't cook?"

"Never know what that woman'll do or say," Jock said. "That lady's likely goin' after a po-lice, tell him somebody back here camping out. Best we move on."

"But I didn't mean to scare her."

"Never mind, boy, we'll cook us something up the road a piece."

It took both of them to pull the gitaway box up the embankment and back onto the roadside drive. Jock spattered cold water on his face and wiped his coat sleeve across it. Then he drank. Chris dipped his hand into the water and dabbed at his eyes, then he took a mouthful. "Let's go," Jock said.

They took to the shoulder on the opposite side of the road, walking unhurriedly while they chewed and swallowed the dry and almost crisp bread. "Sure would like a bowl of cereal," Chris said.

"Coffee'd be good, too," Jock said, "an' we'll have some 'fore the day's over."

For an hour they trudged up the winding hillside road, staying well away from the path of the oncoming cars, not once looking back. "Sure wish we had a car," the boy said once.

"Wouldn't do no good. Paw-paw can't drive."

"My daddy could."

They walked on silently then.

They passed an old log house built on the side of the road and close to the edge of the mountain; it looked like a hard gust of wind would send it banging and shattering into the valley below. They passed the broken remains of a little boat that had apparently fallen from the top of a car. At the crest of the mountain, they paused to let a trailer truck work its way back onto the highway, and they stopped beneath the overpass where a sign saying Blue Ridge Parkway pointed another direction.

They started down the other side of the mountain, then. They were a good mile along the way toward Waynesboro, and there was no traffic at all, when they heard a woman's yell up around the bend. Chris stopped. "That same woman?"

Jock shook his head. "T'ain't the same. The other'n sounded like a stuck hog; this'un sounds like a body hurt."

Beyond a clump of woods at the curve they saw her and she saw them at the same time. A pickup truck with a trailer hitched to it was on another of the pull-offs. The woman started running toward them, waving her arm frantically. "Help!" she cried. "Please help me!" They hurried on, and Jock went ahead to meet her.

The woman grabbed his arm. "Come help me! Please!"

"What's the matter, ma'am?"

"My baby, my husband!" She pointed off the road. "They're down there. A snake's there too. I don't know what to do, but somebody has to help. Please," she said.

Her words didn't make clear sense, but Jock listened through them to the frantic cry underneath. "Boy, pull the box on." He started after the woman. At the rock wall retaining the pull-off, Jock looked down into the brush and heavy boulders. Squatting and half leaning against the stump of a storm-splintered tree was a curly haired little girl, no more than three, her little hands clutched to her chest, whimpers coming from her quivering lips. Across a shallow ravine, a man stood stock-still, holding aloft a stubby tree limb, trembling with it but clearly unwilling to bring it down. His legs were set, his shoulders were hunched.

Between them but closer to the child and partially hidden by the edges of a jutting rock was a nerve-taut snake, head rocking, tongue stabbing at the air. A moccasin, Jock thought. Mocccasins had no business up this high, but there it was.

"Mister," Jock said, "don't move." The man looked up. "Don't move none," Jock said. "Talk to your baby. Talk to 'er, keep 'er easy."

He turned about and jerked open the side of the gitaway box, plucked out the slingshot, and scattered the tools and fishing lines tucked in beside it. He fumbled on the ground for three stones about the size of marbles, kicking the gravel away to make sure he got the best ones.

He placed one of the stones in the leather pocket and flexed the rubber thongs. Should of tested it 'fore now, he thought, should of. He glanced across the road and spotted a tin can half hidden in the grass.

"Mister, you can't do anything with that."

"Got to' ma'am, just got to."

He put on his glasses and took careful aim, pulled

back till the thongs were stretched as far as he dared, held a moment, then let go. The pocket made a slapping sound as it struck the stock, but that sound was quickly lost in the clang sound of the rock striking the can. The target whirled off to one side and came to rest with the round end facing him. Once more Jock put a rock in the pocket, once more he drew back and aimed. And once again a rock clanged against tin.

"One thing to hit a can," the woman said, "another to hit a live snake. You can't do it, mister."

"Got to do it," Jock repeated.

He stepped back to the retaining wall and looked down. "Mister," he called, "keep talkin'. Soon's I hit that snake, you grab your baby."

"You got a gun?" The man didn't look up.

"A slingshot," Jock said.

"Slingshot," the man said. "Nobody could hit a snake that far with a slingshot. Honey, you get somebody else."

"Never mind, ma'am," Jock said, "I can hit it. Mister, you see to your baby when I say."

Again he loaded the pocket and drew back. He squinted down at the snake's head, stared at it till the carried-over image of the round tin can top circled it. He turned loose and watched the rock smash away half of it. "Now! Get'er now!"

The man dropped the limb across the writhing snake's body and made a sweeping, clutching grab for the child. He scrambled up the bank, digging in toes and knees and one free hand. At the edge of the wall he sat down and hugged the girl to him.

"Thank God," the woman sobbed, "thank God, thank God, thank God!"

Jock turned about and handed the slingshot to Chris. "Seen better ones, but it'll do."

"Paw-paw, I never saw anybody shoot one that good. Guess you could kill a squirrel or a rabbit, maybe even a bird while it's flying."

"I'll learn you," Jock said."We get to Bucksville an' I'll learn you." Unhurried now, he replaced the weapon in the gitaway box and put the lines and tools back in order.

The man gave the child to her mother and came over. "Mister, I've seen fancy gun shooting, pretty fair shot myself, but I never saw the likes of that." He caught Jock's hand and shook it hard. "Thanks isn't big enough, but thanks anyway."

"It'll do," Jock said. He crossed over to where the mother and child still sat on the gravel. He stooped down and touched the little girl's chin. "Biddie," he said, "was you scared?" There were no tears in the child's eyes, but her face was white. Dumbly she nodded. "Been me, I'd of been scared more'n you," Jock told her. "My but you're pretty. Ain't she pretty, boy?" Chris came up and stood uncertainly and nodded.

After a moment Jock turned and looked back at the gitaway box. "Boy, reckon we better get goin'. Folks here's all right now."

"You walking?" the man asked.

"That's right, mister," Jock said.

"How far are you going?"

"Far as we can get 'fore sundown."

The man glanced at his wife and at the truck and back at Jock. "Best I can offer is the bed of the pickup, but you're welcome to that as far as we go."

Jock saw the quick look in Chris's eyes. "Which way you headed?"

"About ten miles the other side of Waynesboro, got a place not far from the interstate route, little farm, nothing big. I work in town but I like ground around me. You can sure ride that far if you don't mind the truck bed."

"Ground's a good thing to have," Jock said, "an' the truck don't bother us none, does it, boy?"

"I'd like to ride in a truck," Chris said.

Together they put the gitaway box over the side and turned it so the wheels wouldn't let it roll forward or back. "Say, mister," Jock said, "looks like you done left some tools on the ground. Reckon they're yours, ain't mine."

"Oh, that's right," the man said. "I forgot about them. I was tightening the trailer hitch when Carol hollered that Nancy was down in the woods." He put them in the toolbox at the back of the cab. "Ready?"

"Reckon so," Jock said. "Boy, you hold on good."

The man drove cautiously down the mountainside, and when they came to the town of Waynesboro he had to work his way through uneven lights and traffic stops to the route taking them west. At first, Chris sat on the edge of the truck bed, but after the first three or four miles he slid down to the floor and leaned back against the gitaway box and looked at his grandfather. "Not so comfortable back here."

"Trucks ain't made for comfort, but it beats walkin', don't it?" Jock smiled.

"Guess it does," Chris agreed.

Beyond the city, the land was open and clear, and though the road was narrow there was little traffic. The trailer bumped along noisily behind and talking wasn't easy. Jock spent the time looking out at the fresh growth of young corn and what he took to be tobacco. He wasn't sure about the latter, though, cotton he'd have been certain of. If he could just say Alabama instead of Virginia and if the fences were a little more weatherworn and there weren't an occasional field where horses roamed, he could easily think this was Bucksville country. He closed his eyes and halfway wished it were.

"Paw-paw, I'm getting hungry."

Jock opened his eyes and glanced toward the gitaway box. He thought about the leftover cookies. "Tell you what, boy, soon's we get down the road a-ways, Paw-paw'll cook up them eggs and brew us some coffee."

"I don't want breakfast in the middle of the day," Chris said. "Don't we have anything else?"

"There's a can of spaghetti or some such an' some pork an' beans, an' there was a can of peaches your ma had, I brung that with us."

Chris looked off toward the fields they were passing.

"Don't sound good. Wish we could eat something else at a table somewhere."

In his pocket Jock had all the money they owned in the world, $23.70, not enough to carry them as far as they had to go. "You mean a ca-fe?"

"That or a house."

"Ain't no house," Jock said. "But we'll see, maybe down the road from where we get out there'll be something, store or ca-fe or some such. How'd you like that?"

"Be better'n spaghetti or pork and beans," Chris said. "I never did like those beans."

"Get hungry enough, you'd like 'em," Jock said.

The man slowed down in the wide open country and pulled off onto a winding driveway. Up ahead was a small white house, half hidden by a curving row of evenly spaced cedars. Carefully placed plantings marked the gravel drive. The man stopped and got out. "Far as we go," he said. He took a ten dollar bill from his wallet and pressed it toward Jock.

Jock climbed down and helped Chris with the gitaway box. "Much obliged, mister," he said, "but the ride's good enough."

"You sure?"

"I'm sure," Jock said. He turned the box about and handed Chris the handle. "Me an' the boy'll make it from here."

"Mind telling me how far you're going?"

Jock had never thought it wise to speak his business, not even to kin and especially not to unkin. "A piece.

We'll make it."

"We'll never forget what you did, " the man said.

His wife got out the other side and came around. "Sure won't, " she added. "Wherever you're going, we wish you well."

"Much obliged, ma'am." Jock shook hands. "Come on, boy, the day's gettin' shorter."

Once out of earshot, Chris looked at his grandfather. "They meant you to have that money."

"Pay for pay, that's all we got comin'," Jock said. "We done 'em a turn, they done us one. Take more'n your due, folks'll lose respect for you."

"That ten dollars would have bought us a bus ticket to the next town," Chris said.

"Sure's we took it, the bus'd break down an' we'd have to walk anyhow," Jock said. He trudged along the roadside and gave the boy a hand with the gitaway box. "Maybe 'round the next curve'll be a ca-fe," he said. "You still hungry?"

"Hungrier than I was."

The cafe was around the third curve away, a narrow and weather-battered structure next to an aging gas station, not advertised except by a small black and white hand-lettered sign over the door saying BAR-B-Q & LUNCH.

"Ain't much to look at," Jock said.

"You're sure we can go inside?" Chris asked.

"Door's open an' there's folks, I see 'em."

"Wish there was a better one."

"Ain't though," Jock said. "Mightn't be another'un in

the next ten miles. This ain't one of the big roads, 'cording to the map, just country."

The inside was dark and brownish, its unmoving air permeated by the odor of stale beer and boiling kraut. A beaten counter ran from the door all the way back to a kind of partition that separated the dining room from the kitchen. The separation was only partial, however, and the steam and heat came through it to a window fan hardly big enough to serve the smallest bedrooms.

"I don't like this place, Paw-paw."

"We didn't come to look, come to eat," Jock said. The boy held the screen door open while his grandfather tugged at the gitaway box.

A man with a half-burnt cigarette stuck in the corner of his mouth, a kind of cup towel wrapped around his head, and a stained apron around his waist came forward from the far end of the counter. "Mister, don't bring that thing in here. Got no room for it."

Jock glanced at the three empty tables and the two customers at the counter, one of them wearing overalls and a blue shirt, and the other dressed in a shiny blue serge suit. "Can't leave it on the road. Got all our belongin's in it."

"You can't bring it in, neither," the man repeated. "Bad enough folks bringin' in suitcases. Sure ain't havin' a wagon dragged in, bustin' up the tables."

Jock looked at the man and at Chris and at the man again. "Come on, boy." He pulled the box outside again.

"But, Paw-paw, I'm hungry."

"So'm I," Jock said, "but you heard him; he don't like

carts." He glanced at the door. "But he ain't got nothin' against suitcases." He cocked up the front of the gitaway box and undid its brackets, removing the wheels. He took apart the wing nut and bolt and disengaged the handle. Without haste, he opened the box's side and placed both within.

When he walked back in the cafe, he carried the box like a hand grip. "I told you—" the man began.

"Nothin' but a homemade grip." Jock said, and without hesitation he carried it to one of the tables and sat down. "Lunch sign says you got winnies an' kraut an' string beans. What's the charge?"

"What it was on the sign, ninety-five cents."

"You charge extry for drinkin' water?"

"Comes with the plate," the man said, "coffee or milk's extra."

"How much you want for coffee?"

"Five cents with the plate, a dime by itself."

"Paw-paw, I don't want coffee, I'd rather have milk."

"How much is your milk?" Jock asked.

"Little glass ten cents, big'un is fifteen."

"Bring us a coffee an' a big milk, an' two plates."

"You want bread or rolls?"

"I'd like rolls, Paw-paw."

"Rolls for both," Jock said.

Never mind the way the man talked, and never mind the dimness of the place, the plates were filled to overflowing and the glass of milk was a big one, no doubt about it. The man was indifferent about how he put them on the table, however, letting juice from the kraut spill off one plate and tipping the milk so that part of it poured onto the table and dribbled to the floor. "Been better if you'd come to the counter," the man said. He took the tail end of his apron and wiped the table, then he went back to the kitchen and got a mop and dabbed at the floor.

Jock dug in. Chris went at it more slowly, gingerly tasting the kraut. "Sure is a different kind of dinner," he said.

"Out-of-the-way place like this," Jock told him, "don't put on airs. Terrible price, though, for winnies an' kraut an' beans." He broke open one of the rolls and bit into it. "Beans is good, put meat on your bones."

They were half finished when the screen door banged open again and a man of medium build stomped in. A day's growth of beard clouded his face, and a smear of grease made a jagged line across his chin. His coat was to one side, bottom button in the top buttonhole, and the knot in his tie was pulled under one collar point. The soiled felt hat looked like it had been sat upon, then pushed into a new shape, with the brim canted over the left ear and pulled down on the other side. The man behind the counter looked up. "Les Purdey, I told you not to ever come in here no more drunk."

"Ain't nobody drunk," the man said. "Coupla sniffs, nothin' more'n a coupla sniffs."

He got to the counter and leaned against it. "Gimme a beer," he said.

"You know I got no license to sell beer on Sunday," the counterman said. "And besides, I wouldn't sell you one anyhow."

The man called Les Purdey looked at the two others sitting at the counter. "Now ain't that somethin'? Got a payin' customer and he don't want to sell to 'im. Ain't that somethin'?"

"Whyn't you take yourself outa here?" the counterman said. "I told you and I told you to not never come in here drunk."

"You done said that. Can't you come up with nothin' new?" Les looked at the customer in overalls. "How come you don't tell Pinky there to get outa here, too? He got on them same duds he wears milkin', comin' in smellin' like the barn, ain't spendin' more'n the price of coffee. An' the deacon over there in the same ol' blue suit he's been wearin' for the last ten years, dressed up like he was goin to a Sunday go-to-meetin'. Bet he ain't spent more'n a dime a day here f'r who knows how long. An' you won't even sell me a beer. An' I got the money, too." He took a quarter and two nickels and put them on the counter. "Pinky, you tell him to sell me a beer."

The man in the overalls slowly stirred his coffee. "Your mouth ain't let up goin' yet," he said. "Tell 'im yourself."

"I done told him," Les said.

"Ain't no use in anybody else tellin' him," Pinky answered.

Les turned about and for the first time saw Jock and Chris. "Well, now, looky there, got real payin' customers eatin' some of your kitchen slop. Did you tell 'em how old them winnies was? An' that other awful-smellin' stuff—rotten cabbage, ain't it?—oughtn't charge nobody for stuff like that." He pushed himself uncertainly from the counter and ambled closer to their table. "Y'all ain't been through here b'fore. Folks that know better wouldn' eat none of Frank's cookin'." He put both hands on the table and leaned forward, peering at Jock then at Chris. "Ol' man, is this yo' boy? My, you got a fine-lookin' one." He brought his face down close to Chris's. "Don't make sense, old codger like you the father of a good-lookin' young'un like him."

Chris leaned away. "He's my grandfather," he said slowly.

The man looked at Jock then back at the boy. "Now ain't that somethin', boy your age traipsin' around with this ol' coot. Ought to be in church with your ma an' pa. Where's your ma an' pa, boy, lettin' you come in a rundown dump with this here old man?"

Jock turned just enough to get good leverage and slapped the man as hard as he could across the face. The man staggered back and tripped over a chair and stumbled against the side of the counter and fell sprawling on the floor. For a stunned moment he sat there, gingerly touching his cheek. "You ol' coot! Ain't nobody goin' to slap me, not nobody, you hear."

Jock reached behind him and retrieved the wagon tongue handle and pointed it toward the man. "Mister, I don't care how many bottles of beer you got money to pay for. You get outa here an' don't you come back inside this here place till me an' the boy git gone, you hear me?

Else I'll bend this thing over that thick skull of yours, you hear me good."

Slowly the man sat up. "Why, you ol' coot—"

"You keep a civil tongue in your head," Jock said, "stop your bad mouthin' 'fore the boy." He gave the handle a light flick. "Now you *git*."

Halting and fumbling, the man called Les pulled himself to his feet and turned and looked at the counterman. "You goin' to let that ol' fool talk thataway to a payin' customer?"

"Seems you talked first," the man said. "Seems you got no more'n you asked for. Maybe you ought to do like the man said. *Git.*"

Les turned around toward Jock and acted like he meant to say something else. Jock wiggled the wagon tongue. Les kicked at a chair and shuffled toward the door.

The screen door slammed shut behind him. Frank the counterman slapped the counter top and laughed. "Pop, you gave him what he's been askin' for. I thank you for it. Me an' Pinky here, we're younger'n him an' heftier, wouldn't do for us to hit him, an' Ezra's got a withered-up arm left over from the Korean mess. But Les, he's been askin' for it, an' I thank you for givin' it to him."

Jock finished his meal. "Whiskey makes a pure mess of a man's tongue," he said. He reached in his pocket for the worn leather snap-shut coin purse, took two crumpled one-dollar bills and a quarter from it and slipped it back. "Boy, you 'most done?"

"All but the milk."

"Wash it down, then, we got to move on." Jock rose and went to the counter, put the money on its surface. "This cover it?"

"More'n do," the man said. He handed back a dime. "Pop, you done it to him right," he said. "Sure you wouldn't like another cup of coffee? Worth that, seein' Les get his'n."

"No coffee," Jock said.

"Well, how 'bout a nickel bar of candy for the boy? Seein' I spilt some of his milk, he ought to have a little something extra."

Jock looked at Chris and saw the hope in his face. "Reckon he's got that comin'. Thank the man, boy."

Chris got up from the chair and walked across to join Jock, wiping the back of his hand across his mouth and smearing away the milk traces. "Thank you, sir."

Outside, Jock put the wheels and tongue in place and they started off down the road. "Paw-paw, I didn't know you were that strong, knocking a man down while you were sitting. And shooting that snake this morning, too. Don't reckon many boys have grandfathers could do those things."

Jock relished what Chris said. More than that, he sensed the edge of a breaking away from what once was, the beginning of a new acceptance. "You'll do, boy. Here, catch a-holt, we'll both pull it a ways."

7 ....

All that afternoon they trudged southwest along the edge of the wide highway. "Lot of folks goin'," Jock said once. "Reckon they ever get there?"

"Sure wish we were riding, too," Chris said. "Folks come from nowhere and get out of sight before we take ten steps."

"Hurryin's for them that has to. Reckon some of 'em'd like to have the time we got."

At dusk they moved back from the road and around to the far side of a mound that had been chopped through for the right-of-way. They found a shallow creek and Jock boiled water from it for coffee. They had five cracker and peanut-butter sandwiches each, and hot black coffee. Afterward each ate a raw carrot. "They shrunk some in the heat," Jock said, "but raw veg'tables is good for your system, cleans it out."

"Like taking medicine?"

"Somethin' like."

When it was dark they shook open the blanket and slipped inside it. The boy's eyes were closed while his body was still shifting about over the clumps of grass and clod, vaguely hunting for comfort. Jock lay awake, staring up into the night, indifferent to the clear moon and sharp, bright stars, hardly aware of the long shadows of the oak and sycamore trees, conscious only of the aches within himself. It was tiredness again, but more than tiredness and he knew it. The chest muscles drew tight so that he had to force the deep breaths that preceded total relaxation. The hurt was neither sharp nor stabbing, but it was there, pushing sleep farther and farther into the night.

And in the still private silence he sensed the fear of not making it all the way to Bucksville.

Monday morning they cooked the two eggs and had the remaining crackers. Jock went to the creek again for more water. He boiled a pan of it and this time substituted powdered milk for the coffee. "Ain't very much, a growin' boy ought to have a bit more hearty."

Chris hunched over the pie tin and ate the egg slowly, sopping the loose yellow with one of the crackers. "Wish we had some bacon, hot cakes'd be good, too."

"Maybe we can get some fixin's, stop at a store t'day an' get the makin's for some country flapjacks. How'd you like that, boy?"

They walked through the morning hours and it was near noon when they came on the little isolated settlement with its one gasoline station and one store and a battered church sitting well back from the road. Jock parked the gitaway box at the bench outside the store and went in. He picked up a can of spaghetti with sauce and one of sliced pineapple and three cans of hash. In a bin off to one side were a dozen or more apples, fewer than a dozen oranges, and a bunch of overripe bananas. "What're you askin' for the fruit?"

"A nickel apiece an' take your pick," the proprietor said, "but don't finger 'em. That's the trouble now, ever'body's got to finger fruit."

Jock studied the bin's contents and picked two apples. One had a blemish near the stem, but after he'd picked it up he hesitated about putting it back. "An gimme four eggs an' a short loaf."

"Sell you half a dozen eggs."

"Don't need half a dozen," Jock said, "got no room for 'em." Pausing in front of one of the carelessly stacked shelves, he fumbled for the box of pancake mix. "An four strips of bacon."

The proprietor looked at him over the rim of heavy glasses taped at one end to keep the hinge from coming apart. "Mister, I don't know where you been, but don't nobody sell bacon by the strip."

"Never mind the bacon, then. Let me have some fatback."

The groceries came to $2.48. "Keep them two

pennies an' give the boy a coupla balls of gum," Jock said. Outside, they put the items in the gitaway box, crowding the box of mix and one of the cans into the blanket. Jock wrapped the eggs in socks to keep them from breaking and placed the two apples in the little cubbyhole beside Andy's cigar box.

They made almost eight more miles that day and on Tuesday the road was pretty straight, with no hills to climb, and Jock guessed they must have covered fourteen miles. Wednesday came up sunless and overcast gray, with heavy black clouds moving in and moving out, with the air still and humid sticky, the kind to make a man sweat whether he stayed still or moved about. "Rain's comin' up 'fore evenin'. Better move on down the road, come on some kind of shelter."

"Be better if we were at home," Chris said. "I'm scared of lightning."

Midmorning, it drizzled for ten minutes, then quit and the sun broke through. "Maybe it won't rain anymore," the boy said.

"It'll rain. Clouds gather toward the west an' ain't no wind stirrin', pretty soon it'll rain."

The first heavy raindrops came just after they'd finished eating cold hash sandwiches and washing it down with cold coffee creamed with powdered milk. Jock stared hard up the road. "'Pears like a highway overpass of some sort yonder, a creek or somethin', we better make for it."

"We'll get wet before we get to it," Chris said.

"Little summer rain ain't killed nobody yet!"

"Lightning'll kill you," the boy said.

"I been lightnin'ed at since since I was a kid no bigger'n you, boy. Ain't never been hit. Come on."

One hard gust of wind came and swept heavy rain all over them, then it blew on and only a mild drizzle followed. "Maybe it'll quit," the boy said.

"Just rarin' back for a sure-nuff cloud bust," Jock said. "Take a-hold of this handle; both of us better haul it."

The overpass turned out to be a very long kind of bridge over a very shallow trickle of a creek. "Them builders sure was scairt of a little water," Jock said, "quarter mile of bridge to jump a hog waller." They pulled the gitaway box off the shoulder and down under the wide overhang of the three-lane concrete structure. Except for the straggly dried-out clumps of weeds at odd intervals, the dirt underneath was bare clay. Two broken bottles, an old beer can, a crumpled-up and empty cigarette pack, and a weather-parched magazine gave mute evidence that they weren't the first to take refuge here. First like them, maybe, but not the first ever.

Jock picked up fistful of dirt and sifted it through his fingers. "Dry as powder," he said, "don't reckon the road leaks."

The rain came, first spattering, then muddying the dry ground on both sides of the overpass. In a matter of brief moments it came waterfalling off the concrete parapet and splashing down in quick-made trenches. "Looks like a good un, all right," Jock said. He pulled the gitaway box farther under so it wouldn't be wet. "Shame that yonder ain't a creek big enough for fishin'. Me an' you'd have us a mess of bream."

Lightning struck in the woods off to the right, and the thunder noise bounced around amid the concrete pillars. Chris grabbed Jock's hand. His own was trembling. "Ain't nothin' to scare you, boy. Can't come through that road, an' I ain't never heard of lightnin' bendin'—that's what it'd have to do to get us here." He led the boy up the bank a way, closer to where the ground and the roadbed joined. "Stay dry as a bone here." He opened the gitaway box and took out the apples. "Here, chew on this a while, ain't nothin' to match a good apple for chewin' an' thinkin' an' watchin' the rain. Back when I was a boy, summertime, I used to get a pocketful of green apples an' a fistful of salt, climb up in a hayloft when it was rainin', an' lie there, lookin' out an' eatin'. Course, like as not, I'd come down with the bellyache, but them apples sure was good."

"What was the salt for?"

"To put on them apples, boy, took the tart out."

The gust rains had been the prelude. Once the real downpour started, it kept on. Toward late afternoon, the dribbling little creek down the grade began to swell and turn rust red. The dip was gradual and the bank was wide so the stream got a lot wider before it began to get deep. "Maybe them road engineerin' folks knowed what they was doin', a turrible storm an' that crick'd turn into a river."

"Maybe there's fish now," Chris said.

"That water don't mean nothin', got to be there a

while 'fore fish come."

The current began to carry bits and pieces of tree limbs, and once Jock saw a small rabbit caught up in its swell, flopping along the middle and trying to hop his way free. "Looky yonder."

"What's he trying to do?" Chris asked.

"Tryin' to get outa the water."

"Why's he there? I didn't know rabbits could swim."

"He didn't know it, neither," Jock said. "More'n likely water run 'im outa his hole an' he jumped in 'fore he knowed what he was gettin' into."

"Reckon he'll drown?"

"Likely he'll make it outa there. Animals don't give up so easy. Little fella'll keep kickin' till he gets hisself a foothold." Jock chuckled. "I'll venture one thing. He ain't like folks; once he gets outa there, he won't never jump in over his head again."

When the heavier dark came and it seemed that the rain would keep it up all night, Jock turned once more to the gitaway box. "Here, boy, take this here pan an' hold it out yonder where the rain'll fall into it. Now don't let none o' that stuff from the road drip into it; git a panful of fresh rain."

"What for?"

"For drinkin', we ain't got nothin' else." Jock took the half-used jar of store-bought jelly and the peanut butter and smeared some of both on bread slices. No point in trying to cook, nothing for fire, anyway, except the tattered magazine. When Chris came back with the pan of water, Jock poured powdered milk in it and fixed both a glass. "Ain't much, but it beats goin' hungry."

Chris ate silently, washing down the mouthfuls with the cloudy dilute. "Wish we were back home or somewhere." His voice had a quiver in it.

"Boy, from now on wherever we're at, we're home. Don't get any different in your mind." He tried to make it sound easy and comforting.

"You mean we'll always have to eat out like this?"

"Till we get to Bucksville," Jock said.

Just before total darkness closed about them, Jock took the blanket and spread it on the dry, powdery dirt. "Ain't as good as grass an' weeds underneath," he said, "but tain't lumpy." The water sounded like it was spreading so he put the gitaway box as far up the bank as he could, where there was just room to squat down without bumping his head. "Might as well sleep," he said, "ain't goin' nowhere."

"Reckon the water'll get up this high?"

"Reckon not," Jock said. "Them engineers wouldn't like it, rain washin' plumb up on the road." He spread the blanket just beyond the box. "Now, climb in." This time, they got into the sleeping bag with their shoes on.

The water sound was lulling and there was little overhead traffic. Jock hadn't walked enough to hurt but he was tired. They both were, and sleep came quickly.

How long they'd been asleep, Jock didn't know, when the sound of the rushing water and the rain was shattered by the screaming, crashing noise of a car skidding on the road, banging into the guardrail, racing through open air, and smashing slamming into the trees off to the right. Jock woke up in time to see the headlights cut swirling arcs in the dark, then vanish in the water and come to rest, looking like the reflection of two stars. Chris sat up, his hand wildly clutching at Jock's arm. "Paw-paw, what was that?"

"Ain't sure, boy. 'Pears somebody come off'n the road goin' ninety to nothin'."

He pulled himself out of the blanket and crawled to the edge of the roadbed's overhang.

"Can you see anything?" Chris said.

"Can't see but the back end." Jock squinted into the darkness. The hand holding onto his arm began to shake, and Jock thought quickly back to Andy and Stella. "Reckon somebody'll come crawlin' out d'rectly."

The shadowy silhouette of the car began to take shape, and slowly the door on the driver's side began to open. The rushing water was halfway up the side of it, however, and the person inside didn't seem to have the strength to force it. "Help!" a man's voice called. "Anybody, somebody, come help me!"

"I'm scared, Paw-paw."

"Nothin' to be scairt of." Jock crawled out from under the protective overhang and took a step closer to the water.

"Don't go down there," Chris pleaded. "Water's too deep, maybe you can't get back."

Jock felt the current, realized that it was swifter than he'd first thought, almost strong enough to pull his foot out from under him.

"Don't, Paw-paw, don't!"

"Can't just stand here an' let whoever it is drown," Jock said.

"Maybe he'll get out by himself," the boy said.

Once again the door was pressed open, this time a little farther. "Help," the man called again. But the cry this time was not loud—not the cry of someone expecting to be heard. It was little more than the futile sound of hopeless desperation.

"Mister!" Jock hollered. "Mister, you in the car."

The door budged wider. "Hey! Hey, somebody there, you hear me? Am I in a river? What's all this water, these trees? Looks like a wash."

"You hurt?" Jock asked.

The reflection of the headlights dimmed. "Can't tell," the man said. "Can't see."

"You got a flashlight?" Jock asked.

"Reckon it's busted," the man said. "Won't turn on."

"Wait a minute," Jock said.

Chris hugged his grandfather's arm. "Paw-paw, *please* don't go out there. I can't see and you can't, either. If he's not hurt maybe he can stay there till morning."

"Maybe he's hurt an' don't know it," Jock pointed out. He turned about and crawled back under the overpass, fumbling and feeling his way till his groping fingers bumped against the gitaway box. He was surprized to find water up to the wheels. He opened it and took out the flashlight. The beam's thin ray showed that the water was also within inches of the blanket. He flashed the light on the box and found the length of rope stuck away in one of the caches. He retraced his way to the edge again.

"Paw-paw, please don't go out there," Chris repeated. "I'm scared. Let's wait till it's light enough."

"Ain't goin' nowhere till I see what's what," Jock said. Just under the overhang, he stopped and fanned the light out over the water. The car was nose down, with the rear end and the back wheels off the ground. The door was now partially opened and the man was leaning partway through. "You cut anywhere?" Jock called.

"Seems my head's scratched, hand's busted."

"What about your legs?"

"Can't tell yet."

"Paw-paw, I'm scared."

"Reckon that makes three of us," Jock said, "but we can't let him die out there."

"We can't help him." The boy's voice shook.

"One of us can't," Jock said. "Both us t'gether can." He tied one end of the rope to a girder hook, pull-tested its hold.

"I can't do anything," Chris protested.

"Reckon you can try," Jock said. He took the other end and tied it to the boy's belt and lapped it around him.

"What's that for?"

"So's you won't get loose goin' down there."

"I don't want to go down there!"

"You're lighter'n stronger'n Paw-paw. Ain't nothin' but dirt an' mud 'tween him an' us."

"The water's washing hard, might wash me away."

"Mister," the man hollered, "the water's rising. I need help bad."

"You hear that, boy? Here, you go on, now. Paw-paw ain't lettin' you slip."

"I'm scared," Chris said.

"Me, too," Jock said, "but you just trust it to me an' God an' go help that fella."

Chris held back, looked at his grandfather, hesitated a moment longer, then hedged his way into the water. "It's cold, too."

"Never seen it rain hot water," Jock said. He paid out the rope carefully, inch by careful inch.

Chris spent ten minutes working his way through the swirling mud to the side of the car. When he got to it, he grabbed onto the door handle and held it as tight as he could. "You done fine," Jock called. "Didn't he do fine, mister?"

"Mighty fine," the man said.

"Now, mister," Jock said, "grab a-holt of that rope an' work your way up the bank. An' boy, you just hang on tight as you c'n to that door."

It took fifteen minutes for the man to work his way out of the slough, another ten for Jock and the man to pull Chris to clear land. The boy sank down and shuddered. The man from the car touched his shoulder. "Mister, you got a brave son here. I could have drowned down there."

"Grandson," Jock said. "Takes after his pa."

"Lucky you came along," the man said. "Maybe you can drive me to a service station."

"Got no car."

"Got no car? How in thunder did you get here?"

"Down the road a-ways," Jock said. He made it sound vague. "Maybe you ought to get up on the road an' flag somebody to help you out from here."

"Reckon I better," the man said. "But I owe you something, better tell me how much." He pulled a soggy wallet from his hip pocket.

"That all depends," Jock said.

"On what?"

"On what your life's worth to you."

The man hesitated. "Now, wait a minute, mister. I know you pulled me out of there, but asking for pay on what a man's life's worth, no way to figure it. You telling me I owe you everything I got?"

"I'm sayin' no such thing. But you better thank the good Lord we was here."

"The good Lord didn't have anything to do with it."

"D'you know that for a fact?" Jock asked. "Don't neither one of us know but what it was his will put us here when you come bustin' off'n that bridge."

The man didn't seem to know what to do with his wallet. "You're saying I don't owe you a thing?"

"I'm sayin' you owe the good Lord a whole prayer full of thanks. Now you best go fetch somebody to pull your car outa that water."

When he'd gone up the bank toward the road and flagged the first south-bound truck that would stop for him, Chris looked up at Jock. "He was going to give us some money. Why didn't you let him? Might have bought us a bus ticket, and we wouldn't have so far to walk."

"Might of. But it ain't right, takin' money for savin' a body's life."

"Well, maybe he'd have given us a ride—like that man with the little girl did."

"In what?" Jock nodded toward the car. "No tellin' when that thing'll run again, if ever." He pulled the gitaway box out from under the overpass and replaced the rope. "Now come on, won't be too long 'fore him an' some others'll come to pull the car outa the muck. Better for you an' me not to be here." He did not want to answer any questions when the police or highway patrolmen came—and one would come with the wrecker, of that he was sure. "Rain's let up a mite, we'll cross over t'other side till it's daylight."

The rain stopped for almost ten minutes, and in that time they pulled the box back onto the highway and crossed the overpass. At the far end of it, they found a beaten path down the bank and under the structure. Beneath the protective roadway, Jock flashed his light about to make sure it was dry. "Reckon we ain't the first'uns here neither. 'Pears somebody had 'em a fire, didn' use all the wood they gathered. Soon's them folks is come an' gone, we'll build us one an' dry out."

"Paw-paw, you told that man I took after my daddy. Do I?"

"Like one shoat takes after another'n," Jock said. "You look like him, you talk like him when he was a boy, an' you're strong as him, too."

"Did I really do fine, like the man said?"

"You done mighty fine, a real man you was."

Again Jock spread the blanket and they hunched down inside it. "Paw-paw, I'm not sleepy now."

"Just lay quiet, then."

It was almost two hours before the man returned with the sevice truck and, sure enough, a patrolman. The searchlight spotted the car and Jock could hear them talking as they came down to the water. "Good night, fella," somebody said, "you're plumb lucky to be alive. It's a wonder you didn't drown."

"An old man and a boy pulled me out," the man said.

"Where are they?" another voice asked.

"I don't know," the man said. "For a fact I don't see hide nor hair of them."

Somebody played a flashlight under the overpass where Jock and Chris had been. "Don't even see a trace of anybody," the man with the light said. "You must have got throwed out and busted your head and dreamed somebody hauled you out."

"But they were right here," the man insisted. "An old man and a boy and they had a rope and a flashlight and some kind of crazy-looking box on wheels. I never saw anything like it."

"On a night like this, out here in the middle of nowhere?" the first voice said. "Mister, sounds like the good Lord saved you and you don't know how he done it."

"You know," the man said, "that's pretty near what the old man told me."

"Reckon he'll study on that f'r a long while," Jock said to the boy.

"But God *didn't* have anything to do with it," Chris said. "We *did* pull him out."

"Boy, there ain't no accountin' for what God does or how he does it."

Chris lay still for a while before he said, "But he let my mommy and daddy get killed."

Jock took a deep breath and let it out slowly. "Reckon he did, but not 'fore they let you learn what love an' kindness is, an' not 'fore I got there to tend to you. Don't never fret about God doin' the right thing; it's folks you got to watch out for."

It took them a good hour to drag the car from the murky water, and another half hour to get it up on the road once more so it could be towed. When they'd disappeared and Jock and Chris were again surrounded by silence and dripping water, Jock rose from the blanket. "Near daybreak. Reckon we better build us a fire an' dry out these here clothes. We done lost half a day, can't hang around doin' nothin'."

Deep underneath the overpass, back where the concrete and the ground met, they found some rotting wood forms left from the construction. Jock used the leftovers from somebody else's fire to get his own started, then piled on the splintery wood. The eggs were burned and the toast was blackened, but they chewed hard and swallowed fast; and never mind what it looked like, the taste satisfied.

"Clouds'll break by midmornin'," Jock said, "it's good for walkin'. Won't get too hot."

"I still wish you'd let the man pay something," Chris

said.

"You got pay enough, boy, just learnin' you could do when you had to." He put his hand on the boy's shoulder. "Makes a man proud, havin' you 'round. An' never you mind, we'll get there."

8 ....

It took them eight days, sometimes riding but mostly walking. Once they helped a man change a flat tire and he took them twenty-five miles, and once they helped a farmer round up a cow that had knocked her way out of a trailer while it was parked, and he carried them almost twenty-five more. But by the Thursday after they had been on the road for almost two weeks, they were not more than ten miles from the outskirts of Bristol. Chris had read the name on the map. "Can't tell where it is, Paw-paw; looks like it's Virginia on one side and Tennessee on the other."

"Reckon the town musta got settled 'fore the line was drawed," Jock said, "else the folks got to scrappin' so they split up the place. Don't matter none. Sooner we get t'other side, the sooner we'll be outa this here state."

"You don't think the highway patrolmen are looking for us, do you?"

"Can't say for sure," Jock said, "but I know ain't nobody in Tennessee on the lookout."

The road was not as wide along here as it had been farther back; you couldn't see far around a curve for all the trees and grown-up weeds. The path along the road's edge wasn't wide, either, and they had trouble keeping the gitaway box to the side. "Paw-paw," the boy said, and it was almost midafternoon now, "I'm thirsty. Reckon we can stop for a drink somewhere?"

Chris was walking on ahead and Jock was lagging behind, pulling the box. He studied the bedraggled and dingy look of the boy's shirt and trousers. They'd washed them in the creek two days earlier, but the water had been muddy and they hadn't gotten the mud all out. Needed a haircut, too. A boy's hair sure grew in a hurry. Hadn't been combed good, either; looked a little rat-nesty.

But haircuts cost money, and Jock had it counted down to the penny; they had $7.50 left. "Reckon maybe we can have a sody, find us one o' them fillin' stations or maybe a store."

Another half mile and they came upon one of the former, with three squarish-looking gas pumps and two service ramps. It showed signs of growing old, though the frame house that sat back and to the right of it was fairly new. "They have a machine," the boy said. "I see it right out front."

"We'll stop a spell and rest, then," Jock said.

The black-topped drive was also a recent addition, Jock saw, and even though the building itself was older than it looked from back a way, it showed signs of care. At the soft-drink machine he took two dimes from his coin purse and handed them to Chris. "Reckon I'll have one, too."

A short, wiry-framed man wearing grease-streaked light blue coveralls and a black oilskinlike cap came out of the garage. "Somethin' for you?"

"Just a sody. Me an' the boy got hot from all the walkin'."

"Help yourself," the man said. He looked at the gitaway box. "But what in tarnation is that?"

"A box on wheels," Jock said. "Reckon you never seen one like it."

"Never."

"Somethin' new ever' day," Jock said.

A car drove up to one of the pumps and the man went out to it. He pumped gas into the tank and took a five dollar bill and handed the driver change. While he was at it, two others drove in and he waited on them. And a truck came right afterward. The man took care of him, too, before he could return to the garage.

"You seem a might busy," Jock said.

"Busier'n a pegleg fiddler." The man stopped. "Old lady had to go down to Tennessee, her sister's husband died. Old lady usually runs the front, and Hosmer—he's my mechanic—he's laid up with a busted hand from tryin' to box. I don't know what a fella his age—he's goin' on thirty-five—figures to get outa boxin', but he done it. An' here I am, short two." He started toward the car he was working on in the garage, paused again, and looked at the empty oil cans and litter left by the motorists. "Sure hate to see all the trash pilin' up." He glanced at Chris. "Don't reckon the boy'd want to pick himself up a buck, tidyin' up the place?"

Jock looked at Chris. "How 'bout it, boy, reckon we can help the fella out?"

"We're still not to Bristol," Chris said, "and you know what you said about getting to the other side."

"We ain't in that big a rush," Jock said. "Got time to do a turn for the filling station man here." He thought of the few dollars in the purse. "Mister, make it two dollars an' we'll do you a real good job."

"For two bucks I'll want you to sweep, too."

He pointed to a push broom leaned against the side of the building. "Use that, an' there's some old oil drums around to the back, put the trash there."

It took them an hour and a half, and the twelfth car had come and gone by the time they finished. Jock was wiping his hands with a paper towel and Chris was putting the broom back where the attendant had it when number thirteen pulled in. This one didn't stop where it would be easy to use the first pump, and two young men got out. Jock nodded and they nodded back and went inside. "Reckon we're done, boy."

Chris rubbed the back of his hand across his face,

leaving an oil streak over his nose. "Sure was a lot of work for two dollars. Looks like he ought to give us more."

"A bargain's a bargain," Jock said. "Ain't right to dicker after you're done with it." He wiped the back of his neck with the soiled paper.

"Well, let's get it and go, anyway," Chris said. "Maybe we can get far enough to make Bristol and the other side by tommorow."

Jock looked inside to tell the filling station operator they were through and could they have their money. The operator was standing with his face to the wall, both hands held high. One of the young men stood to the side, pointing a pistol, while the other had the cash register open. The second looked up. "Hey, old man, come on in here. Where's he keep his money?"

"He don't know about it," the operator said.

"Works here, don't he?" the gunman said.

"Did a little cleanin' up for me, that's all. Let him be."

"He's done stuck his nose in it now," the man said. "Old man, tell the kid to come here."

"Leave the kid be," the operator said. "I told you all I got's in the drawer."

"Shut up," the man with the gun said. "And you, pop, get the kid in like he said."

Jock called to Chris. The boy started inside, then stopped suddenly when he saw the gun. He clutched at Jock's hand and his own hand trembled. "What do they want?"

"Reckon they're robbin' the man," Jock said. "Just

you be still now; they ain't goin' to hurt you."

"Ain't hurtin' nobody, 'less shorty here tries to get smart. How much money's there, Ellis?"

"I don't count more'n $258," he said. "Thought you said he usually kept half a grand."

"Did when I was workin' for him," the man with the gun said. "Where you hidin' it, shorty?"

"Had to give the old lady $300 yesterday; she went to Tennessee," the operator said. "And you know you ain't goin' to get away with this, Rudy. I know you; cops'll be on your tail in an hour."

"Be plenty of time to get lost in Tennessee," Rudy said. "Take the cash, leave the silver." He looked at Jock. "And you, old man, you go out yonder and fill the tank, hear? And I'll just keep the kid inside till you get done, and don't try no fancy stuff, you hear me, 'cause I don't want to hurt nobody."

"I'm scared," Chris said. "I want to go with my Paw-paw."

"Shut up," the man at the cash register snapped. "Don't want any whimperin' brats soundin' off. I can't stand nobody cryin', you hear?"

"I don't know nothin' 'bout fillin' a tank," Jock said. "Never filled one in my life."

"You ain't goin' to learn no younger," the gunman said. "Now get to it."

Jock patted Chris's hand. "Stay real still, boy. Don't move a muscle. Men with guns is meaner'n snakes. Yella, too."

"Shut your mouth," the gunman said.

Outside, Jock made his way to the car, half looking back and half watching what he was doing. He unscrewed the gas tank cap and reached down for the hose nozzle. He inserted it and turned it on. He watched the door till the overflow splashed out on his hand. He moved the nozzle and fumbled with the cap. When he was through, he didn't know whether it was on straight or not, and he didn't care. He went back inside. "Done like you said."

The man without the gun crammed all the paper money down inside his pants pocket. He walked over to the wall telephone then and jerked the wire loose. "Come on, let's go," he said to the one called Rudy.

"You better not call no cops if you know what's good for you," Rudy said to the operator.

"He ain't callin' nobody, can't without a telephone."

The moment their automobile roared to life and spun gravel wheeling out the drive, the operator rushed to the door. "That Rudy," he said, "never been worth a cent. Robbed me blind an' him workin' for me, that's how come I let him go."

Jock walked to the door and stood there looking out, rubbing the side of his chin slowly. "Them fellas're goin' to be mighty put out with me." He stared at the island in the center of the drive, where the gasoline pumps were.

"*They're* put out with *you,* " the operator said. "Mister, I'm plenty put out with them, every bit o' my cash they got, stripped it clean except for a quarter an' two dimes an' a bunch of pennies."

"They got some of your water, too," Jock said. He

nodded toward the island.

The operator looked at him. "What do you mean, water?"

"Told 'em I didn't know nothin' 'bout fillin' a tank. Got a-holt of the wrong nozzle, that'un on the ground runnin' to the water tap."

The opertor stared outside, then stared back at Jock. "Mean to tell me you filled that tank with water?" He slapped the doorframe and laughed a little, then he laughed harder. "Well, I'll be, I'll be. Reckon they will be put out, ain't a car yet'll go on water." He walked over and fingered the telephone wire and then turned toward the side door. "They got this phone," he said."Forgot there's another'un in the house. If they make it a mile down the road 'fore it stops, they'll be lucky. Reckon I'd better call the sheriff."

Five minutes later, he came back. "Sheriff's onto 'em," he said. "Won't take 'em no time to get 'em. Mister, what you done's worth more'n I got on hand." He reached in his back pocket and pulled out a crumpled wallet, took four crumpled bills from it. "These ones is all I got, but take 'em and welcome to 'em."

"Two's what we settled on," Jock said.

"Man," the operator said, "I'll get my money back. You saved me more'n two hundred. Here, take 'em."

"Two'll do," Jock said. He put the money in his coin purse. "Boy, we better be moseyin' along."

They got no more than two miles down the road before a highway patrol car pulled ahead of them and stopped on the shoulder. Chris stopped and edged away toward the drainage ditch. "Wonder what they want. We didn't do anything."

"Hold down, boy," Jock said.

Two uniformed officers were in the front seat and two other men were in the back. Jock couldn't see their faces, but the backs of their heads looked familiar. One of the officers got out and walked back. "Mister, Harry Brockton back at the filling station said you and the boy were there a while ago when he was robbed." He looked at the gitaway box. "Said he thought we could spot you."

"We was there," Jock said.

"We got the two holdup suspects," the officer told him. He nodded toward the car. "Recognize them?"

Jock looked through the rear window once more. His identification wasn't necessary, he supposed. That operator fellow and the one called Rudy that held the gun, they knew each other; that ought to be enough. Except the law didn't go on one man's say against another; could be a grudge, could be one trying to put it on the other. Jock studied hard. Be easy to say he wasn't sure, had poor eyesight, or didn't get a good look. Tell the wrong thing now and they'd put his name on the record book. *Then* he and the boy would be in for it. Terrible thing, if those people all the way back up there in Arlington would be hunting them this far away.

He stroked his chin and nodded. "Them's the two. The one called Rudy, he toted the gun, and the other'n was with him."

The officer made a note in a small pad and turned to Chris. "Boy, did you get to see 'em?"

"Yes, sir." He glanced at Jock. "The other one got all the money out of the drawer, I saw him do it. The one with the gun called him Ellis or Allen or something like it," he said.

The officer made another note. Then he asked them their names and wrote down what they told him. "Address?" he asked.

"Got no regular add-ress," Jock said. "Reckon here's as good as any to put down."

"Here? What do you mean, here?"

"Right where we're standin'," Jock said. "Where we are is where we be, an' that's where we live at the moment."

The officer scratched the side of his head. "You transients or something?"

"If that means are we goin' from one place to another an' don't live at the first'un an' ain't got to the second'un, yep."

The officer turned to the patrol car. "Mark," he called out, "the old fellow and the boy're just passing through. What'll we do about that?"

"Walking?" the other one asked.

"Mostly," Jock said.

"And stopping at motels?" the officer asked.

"Stoppin' where we get to, come nightfall."

They spent that one night in jail in the Virginia part of the split-up city of Bristol. The guard sergeant chuckled, but when Jock wouldn't let up he finally took the two dollars for the meals they were served, but he said he could not take the two other dollars for the room rent. In the cell with the boy and the gitaway box they'd let him bring along after they'd inspected it, Jock took one of the rags and spent the early morning hours wiping off the window and windowsill, the bunks they slept on, and the washbasin stuck back into the corner. By rubbing hard he was nearly able to erase three scrawled words a previous occupant had inscribed on the woodwork. "Sleep good, boy?" he asked.

"I slept okay," Chris said. "Better than lying out on the ground. But I didn't like it."

"Heard you tossin' about," Jock said. "Never mind, ain't no reason to stay longer. We'll be on our way by midday."

Shortly after ten o'clock the guard came and got them and took them down the hall to a big room with double doors. He led them in and down the side, to a bench at the front. Without speaking, he motioned them to sit down.

"What's this, Paw-paw?"

"Looks like some kind of courtroom," Jock said. "Fancier'n the last one I seen; that was more'n twenty years ago."

At the front of the room, seated behind the high desk, a woman in black was bent over, studying something Jock could not see. "Next case," she said.

A man at a table glanced at a slip of paper, then looked back. "Mr. Ransome, Mr. Jock Ransome."

Jock got up. "That's me."

"Approach the bench, Mr. Ransome," the man said.

Jock stared at the woman. "You mean her?"

"Judge Ringles," the man said.

Jock moved forward and when he was close enough, she looked up. "Pardon, ma'am," he said. "Sorry about your troubles. Sure hope I ain't causin' you no extra work. Told that guard fella no need of him puttin' us up for the night. We'd of made it."

"Troubles?" she said. "What troubles?"

"Them's widder weeds you're wearin', ain't they?" Jock said.

From somewhere back in the corner came the sudden full sound of feminine laughter. The woman at the bench looked up and the laughter died just as quickly.

"This is a judge's robe," the woman said. "I'm Judge Ringles."

"Oh, didn't mean no offense, ma'am. Reckon I didn't know folks in this part of Virginny was so shy of men."

"Shy of men?" The judge sounded puzzled.

"Yes'm. To have to get a woman to be judge."

"Haven't you ever heard of a woman judge, Mr. Ransome?"

"Yes'm, I read about a lady judge in New York and another'un somewhere in the D of C, but them folks do peculiar things."

The woman swallowed and dug her hand into the corner of her mouth. "Well, sometimes people in Virginia do peculiar things, too," she said after a pause.

"Good-lookin' woman like you," Jock went on, "oughtn' let it happen to you. Maybe they ain't shy of men, but they sure are shy of smart'uns."

Judge Ringles coughed. "Mr. Ransome, you were a

witness at a robbery yesterday afternoon."

"Sure was, ma'am, an' I'll be glad to tell you what I seen."

"That won't be necessary. You gave the officer a good account of what happened. Your signature on the statement will be sufficient. It's another matter I want to talk about."

Jock swallowed hard and wished they had not stopped at the filling station for the cold drink of soda pop. "I reckon you mean me an' the boy."

"Yes." She stared straight at him. "You gave the officer some rather vague answers. You know that, don't you?"

"I didn't tell him nothin' but the truth. We done left where we come from, an' we ain't got to where we're goin'."

"Just where did you come from, Mr. Ransome?"

That was the question he had dodged when the officer pointed at it. "Northern part of the state," he said.

"You mentioned the District of Columbia." Judge Ringles was patient and slow. "Could it be Arlington or Fairfax?"

Jock rubbed his hand across the front of his shirt. "Yes'm." He glanced at Chris. "The first'un."

"Arlington," she said. "And the boy. Who is the boy, Mr. Ransome?" Her voice was low, almost gentle.

"My grandson, my dead son an' his dead wife's boy," and bit of answer by bit of answer he told her how they had come to be in Bristol. "But never you mind, ma'am. We ain't askin' for pity or nothin' else. He's my kin an' I mean to do right by him."

Judge Ringles studied her desk top, then looked once more at Jock. "Mr. Ransome, raising a boy alone at your age is a big undertaking, quite a responsibility. Far too much, I'd say."

"Judge, ma'am, not meanin' any disrespect, but I done made up my mind to see he gets to where blood kin is. I already come to ouch-it-hurts, but I ain't come to calf rope yet and don't mean to."

"I admire your courage, Mr. Ransome, and I sympathize with you. But evidently you don't have much money, no place to live, and no means of livelihood. You just can't wander the countryside with a boy his age. Just look at him."

"Yes'm, fine-lookin' young'un," Jock said. "Clothes is a little dingy, but that's on account of the muddy crick water we washed 'em in; an' his hair ain't combed an' it's a mite long. 'Course, boys don't never like to get their hair cut. I'd do it myself but one thing we don't have in the gitaway box and that's shears. But if you think we're just wanderin' the countryside, you got it all wrong. We ain't traipsin'; we know right where we're aimin' for." He turned around and looked at Chris. "We'll get there, too, won't we, boy?"

"Yes, sir." But the answer was uncertain.

Jock turned back to the judge. "An' without no help from the county, neither. So if you'll just tell the po-lice to turn loose the gitaway box, me an' the boy'll be on our way. 'Less you want me to speak for the fillin' station man against them robbers."

Judge Ringles looked at Chris and she looked at the top of her desk and then she looked straight at Jock. "Mr. Ransome, I can't do that. Whether you like it or not, no matter how independent you want to be, the state does have an interest in such matters. We have legal ways to help in such a case. We just can't have a juvenile wandering helter-skelter with a man your age. This is not intended as criticism, Mr. Ransome." She took a deep breath and it seemed to Jock she didn't want to say what she said next. "I don't want to hold you in jail on a vagrancy charge, particularly since the boy is your grandson and you do care for him. But I expect you to remain within the jurisdiction of this court till we can study the matter more carefully."

Jock scratched the stubble of beard along his cheekbone. "Meanin' I'm under arrest sort of?"

"No. But it is the formal request of this court." And before he could say anything else, she handed him a sheet of paper with some notes written on it. "This is the address of the Fellowship House. Officer Lehman will drive you there. Ask for Mr. Bohlen. Tell him Judge Ringles referred you. He'll find a place for you and your grandson until Monday. I don't like to do this, but I have no choice."

"Yes, ma'am," Jock said, "reckon you mean well." He turned toward the bench where Chris was still sitting, then stopped and looked back. "Still say a woman like you's got no business in them black duds. Frill you up some an' spatter on a little foo-foo water, no tellin' what some of the local menfolks'll do."

"Mr. Ransome," he could tell by the way she said it she was trying to overlook what he'd said, "remember—I expect to see you Monday morning."

"I'm listenin'."

Outside the courtroom, Jock and Chris waited with Officer Lehman till the guard brought the gitaway box. Then they started down the hallway. "This way," the officer said.

"Paw-paw, I'm scared. The way she talked, she's going to send me back up yonder, and I don't want to go."

"Ain't sendin' you nowhere," Jock said.

They were almost to the door leading toward the parking lot when they heard click-click-click heels coming hard after them. "Fred—Fred Lehman!"

The officer stopped. "Yes, yes ma'am, Miss Amanda?"

The woman joined them. "Seems the court's got a lot to do these days, making a taxi service out of our police force."

"Part of our duty, ma'am."

"A part I'll relieve you of," the woman said. "You go hunt a criminal or something. I'll see these people get where they need to go."

"The judge said for me to do it," the officer said.

"*I* said I'll do it." She wasn't much taller than Chris but the firmness of time was in her voice.

"But, Miss Amanda—"

"I paddled you in the fourth grade for talking back once, Fred Lehman, and if I have to, I can do it again."

"Well, you know how the judge is."

"I know how she is. Now, you go do police business. I'll see to the Ransomes."

"But what'll I tell Judge Ringles?"

"Tell her *I* took your prisoners," she said.

When he'd gone, the woman looked at Jock. "She's been asking for it," she said, and the soft laughter was like the sudden loud laughter in the courtroom. "Selena, I mean, she's my daughter, judge or no. Wouldn't have missed it for the world—telling her off."

"I meant no harm," Jock said. "Just don't seem right to me, a judge lady. A looker like her, make some man a fine wife; ought to have a house full of kids 'stead of sittin' up there tellin' other folks how to do."

"How right you are," the woman said. "But never mind her now." She looked from him to the boy and back. "Any use in my asking if you want to go to the Fellowship House?"

"No harm in askin'," Jock said, "but we ain't takin' no charity, not from her back yonder an' not from the fellaship place, neither. Me an' the boy, we'll find some chores around town, yard work or window washin', maybe cleanin' up someplace like we done at that fillin' station."

"I guessed as much," the woman said. "Trouble is, folks will wonder why you don't take what's offered. Mind now, I admire your independence, but people these days want without doing. Too many are too willing to let others do for them."

Jock nodded in Chris's direction. "First lesson the

boy's got to learn, an' he's learnin' it good."

"Mr. Ransome."

"Yes, ma'am?"

"I live three miles from town. It was a farm once, not now, but I do have a good barn. You and the boy'd be out of the night air."

"Thank you kindly, ma'am, but me an' the boy, we'll make do."

"Sir, if you'll let me finish. My flower beds are all weeded up, the yard's overgrown, and the man that usually keeps it for me took a full-time job. I need help." She dared him with a straight stare into his face. "For the place to stay and a little money, perhaps you could do about for me. If you mean it, making your own way," she added.

Jock meant it. "But the judge, an' that fellaship man?"

"Never mind. I'll see to them." There was a satisfied look in her eyes. "My car's out back."

Jock and Chris put the gitaway box in the truck of the woman's car and climbed into the back seat. She drove through town and out a different highway from the one they'd come in on. Just beyond a low ridge she turned off to the left and followed a gravel road through a shallow valley to a white-fenced plot of land that looked to be five acres, maybe even more. She let Chris open the gate for her and waited on the other side for him to close it. She drove another hundred yards to a small, freshly painted bungalow half hidden by four huge wild cherry trees and stopped the car beneath the branches of one and climbed out. "The barn's yonder. Tools are in the little shed to the right. That's the pump house to the left. In a couple of hours I'll fix you a bite for lunch." And before he could say never mind, she stared him down. "Part of the agreement. *And* I'll call Selena and Hank Bohlen."

That was Friday, shortly before noon. Jock and Chris spent the rest of the day and all of Saturday working for Judge Ringles' mother. Together, they weeded four flower beds that ran along the front fence and cut measured grooves down both edges of the sidewalk that ran from the driveway to the front steps. Chris climbed up into one of the wild cherry trees and sawed off two withered and dead-looking limbs; and when he finally found the heavy hedge clippers, Jock trimmed the cone-shaped evergreens at the four corners of the house. In the tool shed Saturday morning, Chris said, "Paw-paw, the lawn mower's gasoline motored."

"Never pushed one of them," Jock said.

"I have," Chris said.

"Reckon you can run that'un, boy?"

"We can start it and see." Chris sounded eager.

It took them almost half an hour to start the mower because it had a hidden choke lever they didn't know about. But finally the engine spun and roared and caught. "Terrible heap of noise for grass cuttin'," Jock said. "Reckon worms'd come to surface quick, you run that over the ground."

Chris spent four hours cutting the grass, and all the while Jock raked away at the gravel roadbed and took a can of creosote and dabbed with a brush at the bottoms of the fence posts.

Late Saturday afternoon, Mrs. Ringles came out and stood on the sidewalk in the middle of the yard, inspecting with a practiced eye. "Seems you've done yard work before," she said.

"Not much. Never cared a heap for flowers. Folks say they look pretty, but me, I'd as soon look at a field of corn fresh out of the ground."

"All the same," Mrs. Ringles said, "the beds look neat, weeds all gone, grass edged the way it ought to be. You know, that's the trouble today, you hire these people, never mind what you want them to do, they're always in a hurry to get done and get whatever's coming to them. They'll leave sprigs of weeds, loose grass here and there. Oh, they work, mind you, but they don't have any concern."

Jock wiped his thumb on the side of his trousers. "Yes, ma'am, looks to me we got done what you asked."

"You seem to," she said. She watched Chris a moment, off in the far corner working the mower around a huge elm. "Mr. Ransome," she said, and she tried to say it in a low voice, "I didn't quite get what happened, why Selena was talking about Arlington and all."

"The boy's ma an' pa got killed in a car."

"An only child?"

"Yes'm, terrible thing, leavin' a young'un with nobody near but a wore-out old man."

"And you're taking him somewhere?"

"To Bucksville down Alabama way, got a daughter there. 'Course, she's got a house full of young'uns of her own, but I reckon she'll make room for one more, seein' it's her brother's boy."

"None of my business," the woman said, "but couldn't you have ridden the train or the bus?"

"Takes money," Jock said, "more'n we had."

"Wouldn't the county people help?"

"Didn't ask 'em." Jock rolled the paint brush in a piece of paper. "This here got left to dry. Ought to be stuck in coal oil or turpentine, if you got any."

"Maybe you can find some in the shed," she told him. She seemed thoughtful.

Jock turned his back to her and busied himself with picking up the tools. She seemed nice enough. Trouble was, you never knew. She might be asking to tell that judge daughter of hers what he was thinking. Oughtn't have said Bucksville.

"Mr. Ransome."

"Yes, ma'am." He didn't turn.

"I have some shears if you want to clip the boy's hair a bit."

"Be much obliged," Jock said. "Ain't much at barberin', but maybe I can get rid of the mangy look."

"And Mr. Ransome, looks like tomorrow'll be a right nice day."

"Yes, ma'am."

"Too bad, on a nice day not to be doing what a body'd like. That's how us folks in Tennessee do."

Jock glanced at her. "This here's Tennessee?"

"Crossed the Virginia line coming out of town. And I don't guess anybody in Tennessee would care what folks up in Arlington, Virginia think."

She brought out the clippers. When Jock and Chris had put away the rake and shovel and mower and after Jock had taken a battered tin can and poured it half full of turpentine from a jug he'd found and put the paint brush in it, he sat Chris down on a milk pail turned upside down and scissored away at the long, unruly hair. "Ain't good as they do at a reg'lar shop, but it beats nothin'," he said.

"Don't care," Chris mumbled. "Don't care how it looks. We got to go back to that judge, and it don't make any difference. She's going to send us up yonder."

Jock stared off at the western skyline where a ridge rose up and black against the approaching sunset. "Reckon we ain't. We done got out of Virginny. This here's Tennessee, an' ain't nobody in Tennessee lookin' for us. Don't reckon these here folks care what we do."

Chris turned around quickly and his eyes got big. "You mean that lady won't send us to the judge?"

"Me an' you'll just move on, come sunup t'morra. And she won't try to stop us." Jock looked toward the house where Mrs. Ringles was and he rubbed at the side of his neck with the scissors.

"You're sure she won't?"

"I'm sure of it."

They took an old pan from the barn and filled it with water from the outside tap and took it back inside. It was hardly enough to bathe in, but they made do, getting the grime and dirt from their hands and faces. Jock made the boy wash his arms and legs, too, against the red bugs that might have gotten on him while he was mowing the grass. They'd just finished when Mrs. Ringles came to the side of the barn and knocked on the paling. "Mr. Ransome, there's some leftover fried chicken; nothing to do but throw it away. Think you and the boy'd like it?"

Chris looked at Jock and said please with his eyes. Jock got up and went to the slat door. "Mighty kind of you, so long as you take it out of our pay."

She looked him straight in the face and there was a kind of twinkle in her eyes. "I mean to do just that."

For one more night they slept on straw with the gitaway box parked just inside the door. Once during the night Jock halfway awoke and was sure he heard something, but whatever it was became very still and after a moment he drifted off to sleep again.

Just before dawn, when the first gray streaks were beginning to make distinct black shadows of trees and buildings, he woke up again. "Boy," he said, keeping his voice low, "time to go."

Chris turned and snuggled down and turned again. "It's dark out."

"Time to go, all the same," Jock said. Chris slipped out of the blanket and put on his shoes. Jock folded the blanket and put it in the box.

"Can't see which way to go," the boy said.

"Sun's to the east, a bit north of," Jock said, "and we go south of west."

"I don't know what that means."

"It'll get us away from these parts," Jock told him.

He opened the slat door carefully so the old hinge

wouldn't creak, and they pulled the gitaway box out behind them, keeping the wheels off the gravel. "Reckon that lady'll see us?" Chris asked.

"I reckon she might, but make like you think she won't." She'd be making like she didn't see them, either, he guessed.

They turned away from the rise in the road and headed down a slight grade. Half a mile ahead, the highway made a bend to the left and started gradually up an incline. "That was a nice lady," Chris spoke up suddenly. "A shame that judge lady didn't take after her."

In the half dark, Jock smiled. The boy'd learn.

"I wish we had something to eat, though," Chris went on.

"Come to a pullin'-off place," Jock said, "we'll stop an' cook us up somethin'."

"We may pass one, dark as it is," the boy said.

"Reckon not, day's comin' on fast."

They weren't the first to stop and think of building a fire at the little parkway rest stop. Whoever had been there before had left more sticks and branches than one little fire called for. "Boy, run back to that crick we just come over an' bring us some water for boilin'. Coffee'd do fine on a day like this."

Chris turned around and started away, but he stopped suddenly and looked at the gitaway box. "Paw-paw, there's something stuck here."

The light blue envelope taped on the side of the box had blended so that in the bare light it had not been clearly visible. Now it was. Jock opened it and some money fell on the ground. The note inside was handwritten: *Mr. Ransome–I guessed you'd go. Don't blame you one whit, in your shoes I'd do the same. But you and your grandson are due your pay, so here it is. I figured twenty dollars would be about right for the time. Four dollars and twenty-five cents from that for food and shelter would come to fifteen dollars and seventy-five cents. Business is business, and I guess that's the way you want it. It is refreshing to know that some people are still independent. And if Selena doesn't understand that, she's not the daughter I think she is–beneath those "widder weeds."*

God bless you to your journey's end.

Amanda Ringles

9 ....

On Sunday they walked almost to Kingsport and at dusk they found a small stream about a mile and a half or two miles from the city's outskirts. They made camp in a tight little weedy spot near the stream's bank, almost surrounded and fully hidden from the road by a thicket of young persimmon trees. On Monday they went along Kingsport's fringe route and made almost twelve miles. Jock liked to make fifteen at least, but two brief showers made them look for shelter—once in an abandoned barn, and once beneath the thick and almost waterproof branches of an aging oak tree. On Tuesday they got to a little village called Rogersville. Passing through it, Jock said, "Looks like they run this here road plumb through folks' yards, ain't hardly room for two big trucks to squeeze past one 'nother." Once, when two trucks did seem to come together, they pulled the gitaway box up on a residential sidewalk, it was that narrow. "Reckon these folks never get a good night's rest."

"I wouldn't like to live along here," Chris said.

Wednesday started out hot, like the warm evening of the day before had held on tight during the darkness so it could get a running jump on sunup. Jock slept restlessly that night, and for the first time in three nights he had to take one of his pills. The tight aching across his chest and through his shoulder made breathing hard.

And it wasn't that he had done all that much pulling of the gitaway box the day before, either. The boy was getting stronger, fitting to the work. Maybe his clothes were bedraggled-looking, and maybe that barnyard haircut was a might untidy, his trousers seemed to draw up, too, and his shirt had no shape at all, not even in the front where the buttons and buttonholes came together, there were little gaps between. But his arms were tanned and his face had taken on a bronze-looking ruddiness. And his legs had a power that Jock had not expected, young as he was. That first day, walking through the town of Charlottesville, he hadn't thought the boy would ever make it to the other side; Jock hadn't let him do much of the box tugging.

Good thing, though, that he was able to do for himself now; time was closing in and the old man knew it. He didn't let on. Just made out that it was good for the boy to tote his share of the load. But the weariness was there inside him.

Another thing he noticed. Before, the boy had clung to his hand or clutched at his arm when anything strange came on. Like that Mrs. Worthington and the man from the Salvation Army, like the woman that screamed at the lookout, like the drunk back at that cafe. He didn't cringe, though, that day at the filling station; he stood still but he didn't back away. And he didn't talk much about his ma and pa, either, like he did the first week on the road, always asking questions Jock didn't have answers for.

So he'd done most of the pulling the day before. All the same, Jock was tired, and when he finally roused himself on Wednesday he thought of finding a place down the road to camp for maybe a couple of days, a place to rest and take a deep breath. No rush, they had no place to be at any certain time. "Boy," he said after they'd built a tight little fire to boil coffee water and fry two slices of bread dipped in egg, "what d'you say to campin' a coupla days? Ain't in no hurry, anyhow."

"Here, you mean?" Chris asked. He shook a beetle out of one sock and inspected it carefully before putting it on.

"No place to camp here," Jock said, "but it looks like down the road a piece there's a lake of some kind, with a river leadin' to it."

"What'll we do?" the boy said. He put on his shoes and tied a quick knot.

"Nothin'." Jock grinned at him. "Maybe fish, maybe you can get in the water for a swim. You can swim, can't you?"

"Some. Learned when I was seven."

"Good thing to know," Jock nodded. "You ever fall offn a boat, better know how to swim."

"Only boat I ever rode on was one Daddy rented last summer someplace in West Virginia."

"We can mostly rest," Jock said. "Don't have to do nothin'."

"If we're not on the road, maybe I can take off my shoes and go barefooted." Chris looked eager. "I'd sure like to do that, shoes get too hot."

"Do that, too," Jock agreed.

They ate and packed the utensils in the gitaway box. They poured the leftover coffee on the fire, and Chris scraped dirt on the embers with the side of his shoe. When the last spark was dead, they folded up the blanket they'd left out to sun for the while it took to eat. "Sleepin' bag stinks," Jock said, "needs a good scrubbin'." He looked over at the boy. "Reckon both of us could stand the same."

They worked their way back to the road and began walking down it, facing oncoming traffic. "Paw-paw, reckon we'll ever get to Bucksville?"

"Or die tryin'," Jock said.

"How far is it from here?"

Jock thought. "Near as I can tell from lookin' at the map, we done come 'bout halfway."

"You mean we have that much more to walk?"

"Figure it the other way 'round. We got half as far to go as we had 'fore we left up yonder."

"Maybe when we get to Bucksville we won't have a place to stay."

"Never mind about that," Jock said. "Yo' aunt Jessie'll see to it you get took care of."

"She has a houseful already," Chris said. It was his first reference to that part of his family.

"So many that one more won't make no diff'rence," Jock said. "Or two," he added.

"You think they'll know who I am?"

"A spittin' image of your pa. They'll know you, boy."

Three miles down the road they were both sweating from the quick-hot sun. At a bend they had to pull far over onto the shoulder to give way to a tractor-trailer that had dipped off the road's edge. "Sure wish we were riding," Chris said.

"Reckon the man drivin' that contraption'd like to be out here goin' fishin' the way we are," Jock said. "Never mind where folks are or what they're up to, most'd want to be somewheres else or doin' somethin' diff'rent." He stared ahead. "Boy, ain't that a road sign yonder?"

"Yes, sir, it says 'Sonny's Ford, One Mile.' " The arrow pointed to the left. "What's a ford?"

"Reckon you left the country too soon, boy. A ford's where the water ain't so deep you can't cross it without a bridge."

"The river must be that way, then," the boy decided.

The going was over a dirt road and even though they didn't see one vehicle on it all the way to the ford, it took them almost an hour to walk it, stopping, the way they had to, to work their way over wagon and logging truck ruts. When they reached it, Chris wanted to wade right in, shoes and all. "This ain't the place to stop." Jock pointed to a faint path leading upstream. "Folks comin' by'll wonder 'bout it. Me an' you'd better head up yonder a way."

"We haven't seen anybody," the boy said.

"Like as not we won't for a spell, but toward sundown, that's when the loggers'll be headin' out."

"How do you know they'll be loggers?"

"Ain't no farmin' in this kind o' country," Jock said, "an' if they was stillin' they wouldn' have no sign back to the road."

In another half an hour they had found the place that suited Jock, a clearing free of grass, open to the riverbank and shaded over by two huge hickory trees. For a space of about ten feet along the bank, there were signs of animal footprints, with not one human print among them. Upstream of the clearing a gnarled old weeping willow bent so far over that its limp branches dipped down into the water, its heavier limbs forming a natural umbrella. The sun, now high overhead, could filter through the foliage but could not bake the ground.

Jock ambled slowly over to one of the hickory trees and slumped down at the base of the trunk. He took the huge kerchief from his pocket and wiped it across his face, dabbing away the beads of perspiration. He removed his hat and dropped it on the ground. He loosened his shoes and unbuttoned his collar. "You hungry, boy?"

"A little."

"Rustle up some firewood, then, an' dip a pan of water from the river."

Chris went about the chores, exploring the ground and the woods as he went. He returned with a good armload of dried tree limbs and bark, then took the pan from the gitaway box for the water. "Seems funny, putting the water on the fire and waiting till it gets cool to drink."

"Got to pure it out, boy, no tellin' how polluted that river is."

"I can't see any pollute in it," Chris said.

"Ain't what you see; it's what you got to figure's there."

They built a small fire and boiled the water and let it set while Jock took bread and made two sardine sandwiches. He broke off a piece of cheese for himself and gave one to Chris. "Sure beats the highway for quiet, don't it?"

"It's like we were in the middle of nowhere." Chris looked around. "Almost like we were lost."

"Folks can be lost right downtown in the middle of traffic," Jock said, "or they know right where they are in the middle of the forest, dependin' on what's inside 'em."

"I don't understand."

"Folks can get more lost with their heads than with their feet."

"I don't understand that, either," the boy said.

"Ain't nothin' hard about it, boy, long as you know where you're headin' an' keep aimin' for it."

"Like Bucksville?"

"Somethin' like," Jock said.

They had one withering apple left. Jock cut it in two and ate his half, core and all. "Now what can we do?" the boy asked.

"You scout around while Paw-paw catches up on his sleep. I didn't sleep none too good last night."

Chris wandered up and down the riverbank, once wading in ankle deep to retrieve half of a mussel shell. Once he found a dirt-crusted fishing pole with only a remnant of string left on the little end. He juggered at the bank beneath a rotting tree stump and watched as a huge bullfrog croaked and splashed in the stream. He climbed a young scalybark tree and plucked a fistful of the green nuts. And he started to step across a trickling branch that was meandering down to the river when he saw a long snake slithering on the far side. He stepped back and turned and ran toward the clearing where Jock was still asleep.

The old man awoke to find the boy squatting down by the fire's embers, poking a stick in them and making black marks on the ground. "See anything?"

"I saw a snake, a long, black one. I think he was looking for something to eat. And I saw an old boat somebody left sticking out in the water. And a frog and a shell. Paw-paw, maybe we could take a boat ride."

Jock stretched and scratched. "Reckon not, no tellin' whose boat it is. Might sink soon's you step in."

"It did have some water in it." The boy dabbed in the fire. "Wish I had something to do, though."

Jock rose and walked slowly over to the willow's shelter. He stared up and down the stream, stopped still and listened. "Ain't nobody 'round these parts. Reckon we could take us a bath."

Chris stripped but Jock kept on his underwear when they eased into the water. Jock rubbed soap on his arms and legs, then handed the bar to Chris. "Go easy on it, ain't got anymore."

"I'll just rub where the dirt won't come off," the boy said. He cleaned and rinsed himself, then watched the sparkling soap bubbles float away. "Pretty big bathtub," he laughed.

"Cleaner'n a tub," Jock said. "Dirt don't linger around to get on you."

That night they heated two potatoes and opened the last can of spaghetti and sauce. They had more crackers than bread so they saved the bread and ate crackers. For a sweet taste, Jock dug peanut butter on a spoon handle and divided it with the boy. When it was dark, they spread the blanket and lay down and went to sleep.

Next morning, Jock made a boiler full of oatmeal and thinned it with water whitened with powdered milk. Afterward, he rinsed out the boiler and made fresh coffee. "Are we going to walk again today?" Chris asked.

Jock was still not rested well. "Ain't no rush. Maybe we could fish or somethin'."

"That'd be keen." Chris looked excited.

They poked about and found a rotting log that fell apart with the pressure of their fingers. The little white worms were small and hard to hold. "But them's the kind'll get us some bream," Jock said. Chris rescued the old cane pole he'd discovered the day before, and Jock whittled down a tall maple sapling. They taut-lined up and down the bank. By noon, they had seven small fish. At midday they ate peanut-butter sandwiches and washed them down with the cold leftover coffee. Then Jock set to cleaning their catch.

"I wish I had something to do," Chris said. He sat cross-legged and sipped at the remaining coffee as if it were some sort of medicinal black draught.

"Make you somethin' to play with," Jock said, "or climb a tree, or maybe swing on a limb like I done when I was a sprout."

"Wish I had a swing," the boy said.

Jock sliced open the belly of a fish and deftly cleaned the inside. "How come you can't make one?"

"Don't know how, and we don't have anything to make with."

Jock scraped away the scales and cut off the fins and tail. "Got a rope in the box. Get it out, I'll show you how." Chris got the rope and turned back to his grandfather. "Now, shinny up that tree yonder." Jock pointed to a huge low branch of the nearest hickory. "Tie one end of the rope to where that limb makes a elbow bend."

The boy struggled up the trunk till he could grasp the branch, then he carefully inched out along it. "Here?"

"Good as anyplace." Jock looked up at him. "Now make a double knot, else you'll bust yo' back fallin' off."

When the knot was snugly drawn, Chris started inching back the way he'd come. Jock watched a minute. "Boy, ain't you never heard of skinnin' a rope, snatch a-holt of it an' slide down."

Gingerly the boy grasped the rope, felt it carefully, let himself down—then slipped all the way to the ground. He looked at his reddened palms. "That burned!"

"Reckon so, the way you come slitherin'," Jock said. "You got to hold on tight, lettin' one hand slip a little, then the other'n. Now, get you a good firm tree limb broke off 'bout so long." He held his hands about two feet apart. " 'Bout like this."

Chris scrounged about in the underbrush till he finally found a shortened log. He came back with it. "Maybe this'll do."

"Ought to," Jock said. He went to where the rope was dangling. "Hold it up here," he said, and he tied the log up where it could swing free a good eighteen inches off the ground. "Now git on, an' keep that log 'twixt your thighs, don't let it slip back under you."

Jock returned to his fish-cleaning.

The boy swung back and forth, sometimes going straight, sometimes twisting side to side. "Paw-paw," he said once, "reckon you know how to do about anything."

"Know how to make do," Jock said. "It ain't always what you got—it's mostly what you do with what you got that counts in this world."

After half an hour of swinging, the boy worked his way

off. He rubbed himself gingerly between the legs. "That hurts after a while, Paw-paw," he said.

"Got a right to hurt, the way you was straddlin' it," Jock said. "Reckon you shoulda made a seesaw."

"You'd be too heavy for the other end," the boy said.

"A one-boy seesaw," Jock said, "but I 'spect you never seen such."

"A one-person seesaw?"

"One."

"Do you think you could make one?"

"Made many a one when I was your age," Jock said. "Untie that rope up yonder an' I'll show you."

Together, they dragged another log, this one about nine feet long, over to the tree. Jock double hitched one end of the rope to one end of the log. He pulled the gitaway box closer and flipped the loose end of the rope up over the hickory limb and down on the other side. He looped it through the box's handle and tugged it till the tied end of the log was lifted waist high, then he firmly knotted it. "Now," he said, "ride it."

Chris looked at the log and looked at the box. "I don't know how."

"Just get on the log," Jock said, "and work up it till your end starts goin' down and the box commences to go up."

"Sitting?"

"Sittin' or standin', don't make no diff'rence," Jock said.

Gingerly the boy tried it, testing his way along the log. When he found the spot where his weight overcame that of the box, he began going down. "Now kick," Jock said. He did, and the log's roped end rose. "That's how you get the fun of it, boy. Hunch it down, then kick it up."

It took him several minutes to get the hang of it. But once he'd fixed upon the right location along the log, he found the ride up and down, up and down much like that of the playground seesaw. "I bet the guys back at school never saw one like this," he said.

"Reckon not," Jock said. "Folks learn how to spend money buyin'. They forget how to spend time makin'."

Chris rode up and down, up and down, up and down. When he tired of sitting astraddle the log, he got off and walked to the end resting on the ground and began walking up, swaying his arms to keep balance. Each time he reached a fixed point along it, the log shuddered and drifted down. "Beats a real seesaw," he said. "Balance just right and you can stop where you want to. Paw-paw, I sure wish I could make like you can."

"You'll get the hang of it," Jock said.

Leaving the boy to his play, he walked over to a clump of young sumacs and cut off two forked sticks. He took the pole he'd fished with and cleaned off the bark, stripping it to the bare wood. He stuck the two forked sticks into the ground at either end of the fire mound, and suspended the stripped one between them. Satisfied, he built up twigs and dry broken limbs into an oval shape so the heat would rise evenly between the uprights. Dusk was settling when he lit the fire at the middle and at both ends. He moved the glowing twigs about till he had a full fire going.

"Ought to have us some pan bread," he said, "but we got no meal." He looked at the box. "Reckon we still got a coupla them taters. How'd you like a baked tater?"

"Be better than more crackers," Chris said.

Jock rummaged around in the box and pulled out two fair-sized potatoes. He also picked two of the brown paper sacks he had carefully folded away. "Didn' you say there was some more of them mussel shells off yonder?"

"Lots of them," the boy said.

"Well, take these here sacks an' go fetch me a bunch."

"What do you want them for?"

"Never mind how come," Jock said. "You get 'em; I'll show you how come."

It took only a few minutes to gather the two sacks full. He brought them back and dumped them on the ground. Jock was carefully sorting through them for two large ones to put in the fire for the potatoes when heavy footsteps caused him and the boy to turn about.

In the darkening shadows the man seemed giant-big and forest-hard. His denim shirt was rumpled shapeless, his black trousers clung skintight to his hips and thighs, and his heavy broggans seemed to crush leaves and twigs and even the ground he walked on. At his waist was a wide dull leather belt, cinched in the middle with a four-inch silvery buckle. A dingy hunter's cap was pulled low over to one side, and the only thing even remotely neat-looking about him was a heavy beard. "Well," he said, "if it ain't a party." His voice was tongue thick and heavy. "Been lookin' for a party." A tattered little canvas bag hung at his side, suspended from his shoulder by a leather thong. "Don't beat a fish cookin'."

Chris was squatting by the suspended log, still holding onto the paper sacks. He stared and said nothing. Jock turned his attention to the fish. He skewered them on the spit and put it in place so the bright flame flickers barely touched the clean meat. "Evenin', mister," he said.

"Evenin'," the man said, "a good'un at that, gittin' to a party." He tramped over and lifted the spit from the suspending forks and looked at the seven fish. "Tasty lookin'uns." He put it back and spat on the ground. "I was wonderin' whar I'd git vittles t'night." He moved to the log and tested the way it swung. He walked over to the gitaway box and fumbled with the latch, opened it, and pulled the blanket out and let it fall to the ground. He picked up Jock's slingshot and tested its pull, then threw it on the blanket. He put a huge hand on the box and shook it, rattling the tools. "Well, I never," he said. "What d'you call this here contraption?"

"It's our gitaway box, and leave it alone," Jock said.

"Don't mess it up, mister," Chris said.

The big man looked at Chris and his lips twisted up. "Watch your manners, boy," he said.

He walked by the seesaw log that was still tied over the tree branch and kicked at it. "Ain't catchin' nothin' with that trap," he said.

"It's a seesaw," Chris said.

"A *see*saw!" The man laughed and the sound was

gutteral thick. "A crazy *see*saw." He kicked it again and the log slipped the knot and fell to the side, almost on Chris's foot. "Reckon it's somethin' the ol' fool there made. He wouldn't know a *see*saw from a dead woodpecker."

At the hickory tree trunk where Jock had rested the day before, he hunkered down and pulled a flat bottle from the canvas bag. He took three hard swallows. "Ol' man, what's you an' the kid doin' in these here woods?"

Jock went on with his fish-cooking. "Travelin'," he said.

"Trampin'," the man said, "nothin' but trampin'."

"We're going to Bucksville," Chris said.

"I tol' you to mind your manners, boy. Don't talk to your elders less'n they say for you to." He looked hard at Jock. "You got 'ny money, ol' man?"

"My affair if I do," Jock said.

"You ol' fool, I asked you a question. I mean for you to answer."

Jock's hand shook as he turned the spit.

"You hear me," the man said.

"Mister, you leave my paw-paw alone," Chris said.

The man stared at him and even in the closing-in darkness his brows looked drawn together. "Boy, you want the back o' my hand?" He turned back to Jock. "I asked you somethin', ol' man. You pay attention; you answer me. I don't like it for somebody to dumb up on me."

"Three or four dollars," Jock said, "no more'n that."

The man laughed. "Ol' man, you think I ain't got good

sense? Three or four dollars—thirty or forty's more like it. You got that much, ain't you?"

"I said three or four," Jock said.

"Don't you sass me none, ol' fool." The man pulled on the bottle once more. He wiped the back of his hand across his mouth and licked his lips and wiped again. He propped the bottle on the ground between his feet. "I could use them thirty or forty dollars," he said. "You an' that snotty nosed kid, you ain't got no use for it."

Chris squatted down at the edge of the brush. When he saw that he could do it without making the man look up, he moved away and squatted, moved away and squatted, inching well into the shadows. He carefully watched Jock, hoping for some kind of sign. A sign of what, he didn't know.

The man snorted and wheezed and blew his nose and coughed out loud and spat on the ground. "Ol' man, how old are you, anyhow?"

"Past seventy." Jock turned the spit once more.

"Ol' fool like you, done lived long as you ought to, takin' up good air other folks need," the man said. "Maybe I oughta just kill you an' take that money. Hurry up, you hear me? Them fish ought to be done by now."

"Don't reckon you got the guts to kill nobody face on," Jock said.

"You ol' fool," the man said, "don't go tellin' me what I got the guts to do." He took a switchblade from his pocket and opened and closed it and opened and closed it, making it click each time. "I'd as soon slit yo' th'oat as look at you," he said. He got up and came toward the fire, and his huge body made a long shadow across the ground. "Here, let me see." He put a dirty hand on one of the fish. Jock slapped the hand away.

"Why you ol' fool! Don't nobody ever hit me, nobody, you hear me? I got a mind to carve my name on yo' belly, ol' fool." He swung at Jock with the knife, and Jock staggered back, tripping and falling over the seesaw log. The man started after him, then stopped and looked about. "Boy! Boy, you come here, you hear me? I ain't puttin' up with you much longer. You come back 'fore I cut yo' gran'pa's liver out."

Chris had been there the afternoon before and that morning so he knew where the little trails were without looking, and where the dirt was and the rocks were. He paused and felt along the ground for what he wanted. He made up his mind and decided to go through with it.

"Hey, boy, you hear me? You better not go after no law. You understand me?"

"Paw-paw, I got the shotgun," Chris said. The bang sound blasted through the dark and scattered and shattered and echoed in the trees. Pellets pat-slapped through the leaves overhead.

"Hey, boy! You better stop that, now, you hear me!"the man said. He backed away.

"Shoot him, boy, shoot his head off!" Jock said. "Blow 'im plumb to kingdom come."

Again the bang sound came crashing through. Again pellets flacked in the leaves. The man dropped the knife and clutched at his cheek. "You better not shoot no more," he said. "You better not, you hear?" He turned around and stumbled over the same log Jock had tripped on and went crashing into the brush, splashing into the water's edge and out again, running and falling and getting up and running again.

"Don't shoot no more, boy, less'n he comes back." Jock hollered it as loud as he could so the man would hear.

When the sounds of the man were swallowed by the sounds of the river, Jock stood up. "Boy, he's gone. You can come on out, an' bring them paper bags with you."

Chris came slowly from the dark. "You knew all the time what it was."

"Anybody but a likkered-up fool'd of knowed the diff'rence 'tween a busted sack an' a gun," Jock said.

"Maybe he'll think about it and come back."

" 'Tain't likely. Fella like him don't think. Time he gets to where he can tell it to anybody, he'll more'n likely swear that he seen the gun. Throwin' them busted mussel shells at the same time, though, that was right smart thinkin'," he said. "Right smart."

"It was all I could figure to do; didn't have anything else."

"You done good, boy. It's like I told you, it's doin' with what you got that counts in this world." Jock stepped closer to the fire. "Fish's done by now; I reckon me an' you can eat 'em."

"I reckon, too," the boy said.

They sat on the ground and ate till the fish and potatoes were gone, and they washed them down with thick black coffee. "Wasn't enough to share with that fella, anyhow," Jock said.

Afterward, Chris sat by the the seesaw log and propped his elbow on it. Jock leaned back against the hickory tree and rubbed his chest. For the first time in three days he hadn't the slightest stitch of pain. "Your pa'd of been proud for what you done," he said. "That wasn't boy-doin', it was man-doin'. Yes, sir, real man-doin'."

10 ....

It took them the rest of that week and most of Sunday to make it to Knoxville. Jock preferred sleeping in the open to staying inside a ramshackle barn or a leftover shack from somebody's once-upon-a time farm. And he had no use at all for an empty boxcar. "That's where tramps an' likker-heads an' no-count runaways hide out," he said. "Sorriest bunch of folks on God's green earth." But that Sunday evening, just after they'd finished two bologna sandwiches each and half of a fifteen-cent, day-old apple tart they'd gotten at a roadside store, along with a can of soup and another box of crackers, a fine drizzle began falling. The abandoned string of freight cars on the abandoned sidetrack was the only shelter they could find.

They ducked under one of the couplings, where weeds grew between the ties and heavy coatings of rust covered the rails and the wheels. "Soon's it lets up," Jock said, "we'll head on." But it did not let up, and after half an hour his legs felt cramped from squatting and the rain looked like it was setting in for the night and darkness was blurring the shadows.

"Paw-paw, maybe we'd better get in the car up there."

Jock scratched at his stomach where his belt was beginning to dig in. "Terrible place for decent folk," he said. "I'd almost sooner get wet."

"I don't see anybody around," Chris said, "and I don't hear anybody. Maybe this one's empty. I'll see."

He took the flashlight from the gitaway box and went along the car to the half-opened double door. The batteries were getting weak and the little glow spot of the light didn't show much, but he could see it was empty. "Nobody," he said.

"Reckon we'd better get in, then," Jock said.

They hoisted and bumped and pulled and tugged, and after five minutes they worked the gitaway box up and onto the boxcar's floor. Jock strained and grunted and finally pushed his way inside after it. Chris caught hold of the metal lock bar and climbed nimbly up and through the opening. Jock took the flashlight and walked all over it. "Ain't a fit place for any self-respectin' body, but it'll have to do." They spread the sleeping-bag blanket and wordlessly went to sleep.

When they awoke the next morning Jock could hardly wait to get out. "Thank you, Lord, for the sun," he said. At trackside they toasted bread over a wood-splinter fire and ate cold cereal from the pie tins. Jock wasted little time getting away from the siding.

"I didn't see anything so bad about sleeping there," Chris said.

They walked toward Knoxville's outskirts. "Never had no use for railroad bums," Jock said. "Durin' the depression, folks used to call 'em the livin' dead; some of 'em was drinkin', some of 'em was dopin', and some of 'em was just plain runnin' away from their bounden duty."

"Hobos, is that what they called them?" Chris asked.

"They's a diff'rence," Jock said. "Hoboin's a way of life for some, gittin' from here to there an' back again. Got reg'lar stoppin'-off places, know other'ns of their kind. Only thing wrong with them, they ain't aimin' to work an' they ain't aimin' to stay in no partic'lar place. One thing about 'em, though," he said, "they don't run off from no families 'cause they don't have none. Not the way them bums do. 'Course, I got no use for hobos, neither."

They reached the edge of the ciy, and the smooth-running traffic along the roads changed to a weird hodgepodge of crisscross roads and changing street lights and squealing brakes and the heavy sounds of engines racing up and moving off and slowing down once more. At one particular intersection a truck loaded with more empty chicken coops than it had room to stack them properly was stopped dead-still right under the light. The driver had gotten out and raised the hood, and he was standing on the bumper peering down into the engine compartment. Three cars, stopped with their front ends only inches from the truck's body, had lanes blocked in all four directions. Jock pulled the gitaway box out into the intersection and stopped midway across the street. He looked at the honking, fast-building jam-up. He shook his head. "Oughta see the pore fella can't help it."

He walked over to the car nearest the truck and tapped on the window. The driver stopped blowing his horn and stuck his head out. "Give the man time," Jock said. "Reckon you ain't helpin' none, makin' all that racket." He moved around to the front of the truck. "Got a terr'ble mess," he said.

The driver sraightened up and looked at Jock. "Mister, I didn't tell it to bust down."

Jock stepped up on the bumper and peered down at the engine. He put his finger down on the warm head and pulled it back. He rubbed the grease across the palm of his hand. "My boy was a mechanic 'fore he got hisself killed. Used to say most folks'd cut out half their troubles if they'd wipe off the crud."

"Don't need no ad-vice," the driver said. "It's this here wire goin' to the coil."

"Wire looks pretty sound to me," Jock said.

"Ain't nothin' wrong with the wire," the man said. "It just won't stay plugged in."

Jock felt the metal cap over the end of the wire. "How

come you don't jam it?"

"Won't jam. Git it in an' the first time the motor shakes it falls out."

"Oughtn't be on the road with it," Jock said.

"Now, looky here, mister, I don't need nobody tellin' me how to run my business. You just go on about your own affairs an' let me see if I can do somethin' with it."

"Maybe I can jam it," Jock said.

"You a mechanic?" the man said.

"Ain't no mechanic, but I've done some jammin' in my time. Had an ol' well crank. Don't reckon you ever seen one of them things, had fancy gears an' all. Bearin's wore out an' I jammed it. Worked near four years 'fore I done anything else to it. You got any pliers?"

"Ain't got my tools. My boy was makin' somethin' out at the place an' he borried 'em."

"Can't do nothin' 'thout tools," Jock said. "Man ought never get on the road 'thout tools." He turned to Chris. "Haul the box over here, an' get me the pliers."

Chris pulled the gitaway box out into the middle of the intersection and opened the side. The skillet and one of the pie tins fell to the ground. "Watch now, you don't scatter the b'longin's all over the place," Jock said.

"What in tarnation is that thing?" the truck driver asked.

"Right now it's your fixin' box." Jock took the pliers Chris handed him and pinched the plug end of the wire. "Now see does that hold."

The driver put it in the socket and wiggled it. "Reckon it's wore too much. Ain't makin' contact good."

Jock rubbed the back of his hand across his mouth and got grease on his lips. The car that was blocked at the back now started beep-beep-beeping, with the driver hollering at the same time. "Feller's a mite worked up," Jock said. He got down and walked back to the rear, stopping at the side of the driver. "Mister, have you got a chunk of lead?"

The man stopped blowing. "What in the world would I be doing with lead?"

"Just askin'," Jock said. "But if you can't help none, no point in stirrin' up them that's tryin'." He went back to the truck. "Boy, scavenge around an' see if we don't have a safety pin somewhere."

Chris pulled out the sleeping blanket and turned it back to the open end. "Got one up here, the one we been using to hold it together."

"Let me have it," Jock said.

Chris was unfastening it when a policeman walked over to the truck. "Mister, you got a real mess here. Maybe you ought to have a tow."

"He'll have it runnin' d'rectly," Jock said. "Boy, gimme that pin."

The officer put one hand on his hips and looked at the box. "*What* in the world is that thing?"

Jock was tired of answering that question. "What does it look like it is?"

"It's the craziest-looking box on wheels I ever saw, and you better get it out of the road," the officer said.

"Boy," Jock said, "put them things back in an' close it up."

"Yes, sir." Chris looked at the patch on the policeman's sleeve and hurried his chore.

Jock clipped the clasp end of the pin, then pulled the silvery wire straight. "Mister, do you know what you're doin'?" the driver said.

"Mean to jam that wire." Jock gauged the plug-end wire cap, then bent the safety pin into a block-U shape. He capped it over the plug and squeezed it hard. "Now, stick it in an' see does it hold."

The driver put it in the socket and pushed it down. It was hard going and he had to force it. When he had it as far into the socket as it would go, he shook it. "Well, it's tight. You reckon it'll hold?"

"Maybe it will an' maybe it won't," Jock said. "Give 'er a try."

The police officer went around to the side of the truck where two drivers were now hollering at the truck driver. "All right, you, break it up." He motioned one of the cars nearest the lane to back away and make a right turn.

"That's not the way I want to go," the woman at the wheel said.

"Here's not where I want to be either, lady, but I'm here and you're going there." He gestured firmly and she pulled slowly away. Gradually he worked clear the lane nearest the curb.

The man got in and stepped on the starter. The engine caught and died and caught again and died again. He stuck his head out the window. "How's the wire doin'?"

"Ain't budged none," Jock said.

The next time he tried, the engine caught and sputtered and rumbled. Then it raced at a runaway roar. The man held the accelerator down and hollered out to Jock, "How about pullin' the hood down?" Jock pulled, but it didn't catch. "The latch's busted," the driver said. "Take that rope hangin' down an' tie it to the bumper. I'm shore much obliged, mister. Reckon I owe you somethin'."

"Say," the officer hollered, "get it moving, get it moving."

Jock nodded at him and turned back to the driver. "Reckon so, how far you goin'?"

"Coupla miles the other side of town," the man said.

"We'll ride along an' that'll be the pay."

"I said get that truck moving," the officer called.

Jock nodded and waved at him. "Takes a heap of patience, doin' for folks," he said. He took the handle and wheels off the gitaway box and stored them properly, then he and the boy raised it onto the pile of coops. "Boy, you stand up there an' hold onto it. I'll ride on the seat with the fella, case he has trouble."

"I didn't know you were a mechanic, too," Chris said.

"Ain't," Jock said. "First time I ever touched a truck motor."

As they took to the center lane and moved on with the traffic, Jock leaned out the window and looked at the tie-up behind them. "Don't take much to stir up a real mess, an' that po-lice ain't none too happy about it, neither."

The truck driver took them just over two miles

beyond the long stretch of fancy motels at the south end of the city. At the first gravel road turning to the right, he pulled off and stopped. "My place is four miles up yonder," he pointed toward a mountain ridge, "an' I'm much obliged," he said again.

Jock climbed out and helped Chris with the gitaway box. "Better see to that wire," he said. "No tellin' when it's liable to bust loose again."

Once more they took to the road shoulder, walking. Chris paused once and rubbed his ankle. "Bumped it on one of those coops," he said. He straightened up and flexed his leg. "Paw-paw, how far have we come?"

"You mean t'day?"

"I mean since we left up there—where we used to live."

" 'Bout a hunnert mile or so since last time you asked."

"I mean altogether."

Jock thought for a moment. "Near as I figure it, over four hunnert."

"That means we still have two hundred and fifty or three hundred to go." Chris rubbed the back of his hand across his face. "We won't even get to Bucksville before the end of summer."

"We'll get there," Jock said.

Six miles down the highway, they came to a fork. Both routes looked heavily traveled and Jock wasn't certain which to take. "That'un yonder seems to go east an' we don't aim to head that way."

"But it says route 11," Chris said.

"Let's stop at that gas station yonder an' see can they tell us," Jock said.

The operator said to never mind which way it looked like it was going, coupla miles down the road apiece it took a bend toward Chattanooga. "Reckon that's the next big town." Jock thanked the man and bought two soda pops from the machine. In the vacant lot next door to the station they found a huge wild cherry tree. They sat in the weeds beneath it and drank the soda and ate bologna sandwiches.

Chris sat spraddle-legged and while he ate he took a green grass straw and made markings on the ground. "Paw-paw, you sure fixed that truck." He drew a circle in the grass, a circle that disappeared as rapidly as he marked it. "My daddy was a good mechanic."

"Your pa was a good man in a lotta ways. You got a heap to live up to."

"But he did get into trouble once, he said so," the boy said.

"Gettin' in trouble once ain't hard, 'specially for a young fella," Jock said. "It ain't what a man done once; it's what he keeps on doin' that counts. Maybe he did rip his drawers once, ain't sayin' he didn't, but you can't fault a fella for gettin' in wrong when he don't know what's he's gettin' into. An' he sure come out of it, them medals he got in the army an' all. An' that woman he married, your ma, ain't never been a finer woman. Your pa done a good day's work the time they got hitched. An' you know one thing, boy, if your pa'd been a no-good, he'd of never got a woman like her to be his wife." Jock patted his knee easily. "No , sir, don't ever let nobody bad mouth your pa; he was a good man an' you got a heap to do to live up to him." He touched the boy's arm gently. "But never mind, I figure you'll do it. He'd of been proud of you the other evenin' when that fella come on us."

"You don't think that man would have really hurt you, do you, Paw-paw?"

"Can't never tell what a likker-head'll do," Jock said. "An' that's another thing, your pa wouldn't never want you drinkin'. You hear me, boy. You remember that."

"Yes, sir," Chris said.

Jock folded the waxed paper around the last four slices of bologna and stuck them in the box. He sipped slowly at the cold drink.

"Paw-paw, did you see all those motels back the road a way?"

"I seen 'em," Jock said. "Costs a heap of good money just sleepin' in them places."

"I sure wish we could sleep on a real bed one night," the boy said.

"Reckon you would," Jock said, "but twelve dollars an' sixteen dollars, that's what them signs said. We just ain't got that kind of money."

"I saw one sign that said ten dollars," the boy said.

"Tight as we got to make it," Jock said, "we couldn't let go of six." He started to get up.

"Maybe if it didn't cost more than three or four," the boy said, "we could do it, reckon?"

"I reckon," Jock said.

He got up and brushed the crumbs from the spot on his shirt where they'd fallen. "Get them things in the box while I take these bottles back yonder."

On his way back to the service station Jock thought about the beds. The boy was right, sure would be a good break to sleep somewhere besides on the ground. Blanket kept out the chill, made the dirt a little softer, but not much. He gave the bottles back to the station man. "You sure that's how to get to Chattynoogy?"

"I'm sure," the man said.

Jock wiped his forehead with the back of his hand. "Don't reckon there's any cheap mo-tels down the road."

"There's a joint down there, four or five mile, truckers used to stop there. Reckon none of them stops now, what with that Truck Haven place back towards town. Terrible rundown."

"What do they ask for a night's lodgin'?"

"Ain't sure," the man said, "but if it's more than a buck a head, that's too much."

"Well, much obliged," Jock said. He returned to where Chris had the box on the side of the road, ready for moving on. A buck a head, maybe they could spend that much, wouldn't leave more than seven or eight dollars, maybe a little odd change, but two dollars for a night's good sleep, it'd be worth that.

"Ready to go, boy?"

"Yes, sir."

An hour and a half later, just around a sharp, banking curve they came on a huge white billboard sign with curved colored stripes at one corner and the words Rainbow Court in black letters across the center. "You said somethin' 'bout sleepin' in a bed."

"You mean we're going to stay in a motel tonight?"

"Reckon we can stand the cost just this once," Jock said. "Like a jubilee, makin' it past Knoxville."

They turned into the gravel drive and walked past six small freshly painted white cottages. "Sure ain't big enough for nothin' but sleepin'," Jock said. At the center cottage with the sign marking it the office, Chris stopped outside while Jock went in. There was a high counter in the middle of the room. Behind it, a woman dressed in red shorts and a white blouse and wearing a green ribbon to hold back her hair, and nothing but open-toed sandals to keep her feet off the ground, was leaning back in a lounger-type chair, watching televison.

"Afternoon, ma'am."

She looked at him but she didn't smile. "Can I help you?" She didn't get up.

"Me an' my grandson's lookin' for a room for the night."

Slowly she rose, one eye still half cocked toward the TV. "Just the two of you?"

"That's all."

"Got one double left," and she handed him a card and a ballpoint pen. "Fill it in." Jock wrote down his name and added Chris's just below. At the line marked for the address he wrote Bucksville but left out the state. He drew lines through the automobile identification section and handed the card back. "Need the car tag," she said.

"Got no car."

"How'd you get here?"

"Me an' the boy's afoot."

She looked at the card again. "Never heard of Bucksville."

"No, ma'am, an' I reckon folks around Bucksville never heard tell of this place, neither." Jock took the black coin purse from his pocket and unsnapped it. He started to take two crumpled bills from it.

"That'll be eight dollars for the night," she said.

"Eight dollars!"

"Eight," she said.

He stopped tugging at the money. "Fella back at the gas station told me it'd be no more'n a dollar apiece."

"I could tell you gas was two-bits a gallon," she said. "Wouldn' make it so."

"Yes, ma'am, but me an' the boy ain't payin' eight hard-earned dollars for a night's lodgin'."

"Take it or leave it," she said.

"Have to leave it," and he started toward the door.

"We don't run welfare here, mister."

"No ma'am an' I wouldn' take if you did."

"This isn't a flea bag, either," she said.

"Reckon it ain't," he said.

"Gas man must have been talking about the shack-up court down the road. Maybe they'll let you have one of their rooms for that, I don't know."

"Well, thank you, ma'am." Jock went out.

"Which one are we going to?" Chris asked. He began

pulling the gitaway box onto the circular sidewalk.

"None of 'em," Jock said. "We got no eight dollars for lodgin'." He caught the handle of the box. "Maybe down the road apiece we'll run onto another'n."

A good half hour later and about a mile farther along route 11 they came to a fairly straight and slightly downhill stretch of highway. Beyond them and to the left a junkyard stretched from the road and down into a deepening hollow. The hillside behind it was covered with rusting, crumpled automobiles, long since dragged out of use. Across from it a weather-beaten and chip-painted sign said *Dixie Care Courts* in gray-black letters. Behind an unkept row of privet hedge bushes were half a dozen little cottages not much bigger than the tool shed back at Mrs. Ringles' place.

"This'un musta been what the fella was talkin' about," Jock said.

Chris stopped and stared at it. "Don't look so good."

"Ain't looks we're huntin'," Jock said. "A bed's a bed, ain't it?"

The straight driveway was part gravel, part hard-packed clay, and the gitaway box rattled over it. They were almost to the door of the first cabin when a man from a side yard said, "Hey, you, what d'you want?"

Jock turned. The man was naked to the waist and knee-deep in a partially dug ditch. A shapeless straw hat was pulled to the back of his head and a half-smoked cigar looked like a smudge of tar at the corner of his mouth. "A night's lodgin' if the cost ain't out of reason."

The man looked from Jock to the boy and back. "Ain't

sure we got a spare."

Jock saw no signs of other tenant guests. He came closer to the man and peered at the ditch. "If you did, what'd the fare be?"

The man stared at the box, then glared at Jock. "What are you, some kind o' panhandler?"

"Just goin' through," Jock said. "Me an' the boy'd like a bed for the night."

"If I got one, it'd be two-fifty for you both."

"Fair's fair," Jock said. He glanced from the pick to the shovel and back. "You got a busted water line?"

"A stopped-up drain," the man said. "Mean to trench it to the gulley yonder till I can get the plumbers out. Trouble is, you can't never get nobody to do nothin' when you need it. Had a man comin' today but he ain't showed."

Jock's practiced eye measured the distance from the gulley back to where the man had dug to. Eight, maybe ten feet, he guessed. "Me an' the boy's done some diggin'. Could be we could do some bargainin'."

"Like what?"

"Like trenchin' it to the gulley for a night's lodgin'."

The man took Jock's measure. "Ol' man, you can't do no diggin' through this clay."

"We can't make it an' you don't owe us no lodgin'."

"Like you say," the man said, "fair's fair. Where's your car?"

"Got none."

The man climbed out of the ditch, shaking his head uncertainly. "You don't never know about folks."

It was near midafternoon when Jock started swinging the pick and Chris began shoveling out the loose dirt. It was dusk when they finished. The man came out of the center cabin the minute he saw them put the tools down. "Little rough at the sides," he said.

"Rocks, never seen so many rocks," Jock said. "Mister, this is sorry ground. A fella'd never make it farmin'."

"Don't aim to farm," the man said. He pointed to the last little cabin in the row curving back toward the highway. "You an' the boy take that one, but I'll have to charge you two bits for the towels an' soap. That wasn't in the bargain."

Jock couldn't be certain, but he guessed the outside of the cabin had not been painted in ten years. Where it wasn't flaking, it had yellowed so you couldn't be sure of the original color. The inside was just a little bigger than the double bed crammed back into a corner, and the bed was the only piece of furniture. Empty beer bottles stood on two rough board shelves that were mounted on the wall with loose metal brackets. And in the corner, at the foot of the bed, a strand of wire attached to the narrow window frames served as a place to hang clothes. The floor was dingy, with only a tattered throw rug at the side of the bed to soften any part of it. Between the bed and the opposite wall there was barely passage room to the closet-sized bath. The bath contained a shower stall jammed into one end and a toilet at the other, with a shallow lavatory bowl mounted in between. "This place sure wasn't meant for no lollygaggin' in," Jock said.

They dragged the gitaway box in, further limiting the moving-about space. Chris sat on the edge of the bed and sprawled back. "But it's a bed. Paw-paw, you know it's been nearly three weeks since we slept on a bed or had a shower bath."

"Ain't kept us from washin' or restin'," Jock said.

Half an hour later, they'd both had their showers. Chris put on a clean pair of undershorts and Jock dressed himself for sleeping in his other clean pair of one-piece, button-down-the-front underwear. They ate three hardened cinnamon rolls apiece and washed them down with tap water from the lavatory, and turned out the light.

Never mind the road sounds of trucks. Never mind the now and then buzz of a mosquito, Chris went to sleep as soon as he hit the bed. And for Jock, sleep came only moments later.

Shortly after midnight Jock woke knowing he had to go to the bathroom. Not wanting to waken the boy, he felt his way to the toilet. It was when he flushed it that the noise came, first a dripping, then a trickling, then a gurgling, and finally the full force of water spraying up into his face from the lidless water jacket. In the dark, Jock grabbed for the handle and jiggled it. The spurting grew stronger, splashing over his face and chest. He turned around and groped for the towel rack, but his hand hit the shower faucet and turned it on. He grabbed for the shower head to redirect it, but when he swiveled it the head came off in his hand and water sprayed through the bath opening and out onto the bed. "Boy! wake up an' find that there light switch. Looks like the flood's done come on us." He fumbled about and banged his toe on one of the water pipes coming up out of the floor.

"Boy, get that light on."

Chris turned over toward the narrow corridor and reached up for the drop-cord light string. The shower stream got him in the face and he hollered. He hit the cord but its switch spring wouldn't release. He jerked on it, and the cord and chain broke loose, falling to the floor. "Light won't turn on."

Jock banged his toe against the pipe again. "Don't never want to spend another night in no mo-tel. Boy, see can you get the flashlight an' wrap a towel around one of these busted pipes while I go get the man."

He went out into the moonlit night, sopping wet underwear trailing water down the drive. "Mister, mister mo-tel man," he called. He banged at the door of the cottage the man had gone into earlier. "Better come out here. Toilet water's runnin' all over ever'thing." He banged again.

The door opened suddenly and the man came staggering through the screen door, scratching and buttoning his pajama coat. "What's goin' on? What's the matter, don't you know it's done past midnight?" he said. "Hollerin' that way, you'll wake up the dead."

"Pipe's busted, mister. Water's runnin' all over ever'thing. Light cord's broke, an' ain't nothin' me an' the boy can do," Jock said.

"That's what comes o' lettin' trash use your b'longin's, like as not you never seen a flush toilet b'fore." He walked barefooted down to the driveway and stubbed his toe on a sharp rock. He yelled and kicked at the rock and banged his toe again. "Ought of give you an' that kid your pay for the ditch an' run you off. Ditch ain't worth it, anyhow. Ain't nothin' I can do till mornin' 'cept cut off the main valve."

"It's got a bunch of water on the floor."

"Well, I sure ain't moppin' this time o' night," the man said. "Anyhow, floor's got cracks; let it leak through. An' soon's it's daylight, you an' that kid clear out, you hear?" He went to the side of the cottage and turned off the main valve.

Chris found the flashlight, then he stood up on the bed and jiggled the light till it came on. He and Jock skinned out of their wet underwear, and Jock found the towel where it had fallen at the foot of the bed.

Chris dried the side of his face. "Paw-paw, I'm not sleepy anymore. And besides, the bed got wet. How come we can't just go now?"

"It'd sure beat stayin' here. 'Most daylight no-how." Jock began dressing. "Hang them wet clothes 'cross the box. Come sunup they'll dry out."

They dragged the gitaway box through the door and down the drive. Once more Jock stopped at the cottage where the man was, and though the light inside was off, he knocked on the door. At the second knock the man jerked it open and stuck his head out. "Now what?"

Jock handed him a quarter. "Here's for the towels,"

he said. “An’ another thing, ought to tell folks stayin’ with you not to leave their beer bottles. Ain’t good for kids to see beer bottles lyin’ around.”

In the gray pre-dawn they made their way slowly down the drive toward the highway, the gitaway box crunching on the gravel and packed clay ruts. “Paw-paw, I didn’t sleep much, all those trucks going by.”

Jock rubbed himself under the arm where he hadn’t toweled good. “No sir, an’ me, neither. An’ if this here’s a sample of mo-tel sleepin’, I don’t favor it. Not none.”

11 ....

Jock did not try to account for it. He simply accepted fatigue when it came late that afternoon. If they had only made ten miles or therebouts that day, well, that's all they'd made. Other days were ahead. In between, they could rest.

When they came on a creek that ran parallel with the road a short distance then meandered through an uncertain hollow and back into the woods, they took to the footpath that followed it. Five minutes away from the highway and they were caught up in thick brush and huge trees. "Like ain't nobody ever been here," Jock said. They made their own camp site by using the blanket to beat down the weeds and undergrowth and rolling the gitaway box back and forth. Chris found an opening in the tall grass and pressed through it to the water's edge, while Jock found an old rotting stump, left over from a lightning strike, and a felled trunk. The fire was just large enough to boil coffee water and heat spaghetti with thin tomato sauce. Neither felt much like talking, and after the night before in the motel cottage they were both glad to be back under the stars. "Don't reckon we'll hear no rollin' freight trucks back here," Jock said.

"And no broken water pipe, either." Chris sopped the sauce with the crust of bread. "Paw-paw, I don't figure it."

"Don't figure what?"

"That creek there, it makes noise, just as loud as those pipes, but it doesn't keep you awake and I can't understand why."

"Reckon there's just a big diff'rence b'tween the sounds God give us an' them we make ourselves," Jock said. It was hardly dark when they slipped down into the blanket roll and went to sleep.

Wednesday the going was easier and they covered a good eighteen miles. Not until late that afternoon, when they stopped at a roadside store for the few provisions they could afford, did they realize the day before had been the Fourth of July. "And we didn't do anything to celebrate it," Chris said.

"Done more'n most," Jock said. "It was Independence Day an' I don't know nothin' more indepedent than bein' where we was." He bought a can of beef stew and another of hash, a loaf of day-old bread, a ten-cent box of vanilla wafers, a quarter of pound of cheese, and a full pound of paper-bagged coffee. Jock gave the man within two cents of even change. When he got the coins back he left them on the counter and took, instead, two wrapped pieces of bubble gum. He split one with Chris and pocketed the other. "That way we'll git two for the price of one."

Near dusk they came onto a shallow branch that had only a trickle of water in it. Jock stopped and pointed to it. "Spring water, sure as I'm standin' here. Bet it's cold an' fresh. Sure would be good to have some cold fresh spring water, boy." They left the road and wound their way along the branch bed for a quarter of a mile. It came to an abrupt stop at the base of a huge mossy boulder. A clear pool no more than three feet wide was bottomed with rich tan pea-gravel and busy with inch-long minnows. "Won't have to do no boilin' of this."

Chris leaned over and watched the minnows. "How'd they get here?"

"No tellin'," Jock said. "Just make sure you don't dip up none of 'em when you git water."

They had just opened the gitaway box and Jock was preparing to take out the cooking utensils when they simultaneously heard a faint gobble-flutter sound. Chris stopped still. "Paw-paw, what's that?"

Jock squinted and stared up into a tree. "Boy, don't move," he whispered. "It's a half-growed turkey. Ain't no farm near by. Must be a wild 'un."

"Turkey," Chris whispered back. "Sure would be

good to eat turkey, Paw-paw."

The low gobble sound came again. "Boy, stay stock-still an' ease me that slingshot." He felt around on the ground for a stone and fitted it into the slingshot pocket. "Ain't nothin better'n a tender-cooked tom turkey." Softly he mocked the gobble. The young bird raised his head and cocked it. Jock took careful, cautious aim and shot its head halfway off. "Boy, get up some firewood an' make me a spit like that'un we cooked the fish on."

It took all of three hours to clean and cook the turkey. They ate it by the light of the glowing embers and drank cold spring water. When they'd eaten all they could, there was little left except the neck and one wing. Jock took those and carefully wrapped them in a wrinkled piece of waxed paper he'd saved from the last pack of cheese they'd used up. "Best eatin' since 'fore we left up yonder."

"Better than spaghetti and hash and stew," Chris said. "Got a lot of mess, though. What'll we do with the bones and feathers and things?"

"Wait'll mornin' an' bury 'em."

"We could just leave them, I guess."

"Varmints'd be around no sooner'n we left," Jock said, "make a mess of this here place. Next fella'd wonder what kind of tramps'd do such."

They slept quietly and well that night. Early the next morning, right after they'd eaten two of the four eggs and the turkey wing and neck, Jock took a short stick and dug a hole half a dozen yards from the spring. He put the bones, the scraps, and the eggshells there and covered them over. "Wouldn' want nobody to think we was careless of our leavin's."

They'd walked no more than an hour and were approaching the outskirts of a town that a wooden sign on the roadside said was Sweetwater when the first driblets of rain gave hint of more to come. "Sure wish we were riding today," Chris said.

Jock looked up at the sky. "Threatenin', looks like it might be another'n like that night under the bridge or whatever."

"Maybe we could spare enough to ride a bus a little way," the boy said.

Jock knew to the penny what they had left of the money they started out with and that they'd earned. Came to $6.81. "Can't spare much, but we'll see what the fare is, soon's we find the depot."

They didn't have to find the depot. As they were about to drag the gitaway box across the railroad tracks just north of town, an old faded blue bus with the words Interstate Freeways painted in bright red on the side rumbled and squealed and shook to a stop at the crossing's warning marks. Jock tapped on the side to get the driver's attention and went toward the door. The driver looked out and Jock knocked once more. The man opened the door. "Yeah, what is it?"

"Which way you goin', mister?"

"Chatt'nooga."

"What's the fare?" Jock said.

"Buck an' a half for grown-ups, a buck for kids. How

old's the boy?"

"The boy's nine. How far'll a dollar an' eighty-one cents take us?"

"A buck seventy-five'll take the both of you to a place called Cleveland, and you can keep the six cents."

"Cleveland? Never heard of a Cleveland in Tennessee. It is in Tennessee, ain't it?" Jock asked.

"Yeah, it's in Tennessee," the driver said, "a piece this side of Chatt'nooga. You want to go, you an' the kid get in; I ain't got time to sit here jawin' all day."

Jock motioned to Chris and they climbed aboard. It took both, pulling hard, to tug the gitaway box up the high steps after them. The driver looked at the box and scratched the side of his neck and shook his head. "That'un beats all."

"It's a gitaway box," Chris told him.

"That's exactly what it looks like," the driver said, "a gitaway box. I never b'fore seen anything to match it, but if I had, it'd been called that, too." He pulled the lever and closed the door, and the bus lurched forward.

Jock fumbled and undid the handle, then he turned the box up endwise in the bus aisle and removed the wheels. The driver watched out of the corner of his eye. "Mister, I've been bus drivin' ten years in all the backwoods places from the Louisiana swamps plumb through the Smokies and all over this state, but I never seen one of them things. Reckon you made it."

"Yep."

"Something you invented?"

"Guess you could say that."

"Well, the day you start manufacturin' and sellin' 'em, I wish you'd let me know. That'll be the day I give up bussin' and go to truckin'."

"I'll just do that." Jock stored the handle and wheels, then he fished the money from his pocket and gave it to the driver.

When they reached Cleveland the rain had stopped and the bright, hot midafternoon sun was raising fine steam from the pavement. Jock and Chris wandered down one side street in the wrong direction and had to backtrack three blocks before finding the route 11 sign again. "Arrows ain't very clear marked through towns, I've come to notice," Jock said. "Folks in a hurry'd sure get flustered." They left the outskirts of Cleveland shortly after three o'clock and walked till nearly six.

"Paw-paw, I've been wondering what day it is."

"Come to think of it," Jock said, "I'd say it's Thursday. Let's see now, we stopped back yonder on a Monday at that mo-tel place, an' we come two days since, an' this is the third. Yep, I guess this must be Thursday."

"I mean what day of the month?"

"Well, we found out too late to do anything about it that Tuesday was the Fourth of July. That makes today the sixth. Anything special about the day of the month?"

"Not the sixth, but the eighth. July the eighth is my birthday."

Jock looked at him. "Boy, that's right, I plumb forgot. Well, what do you know, two days from now an' you'll be ten. You're a mighty big 'un for ten."

Chris looked off toward the range of mountains stretching endlessly to the east. "Don't guess I'll have a birthday cake like I used to. Or anything."

"Well, now, maybe we can do somethin' special, ought to do somethin' special on a boy's ten-year-old birthday. Paw-paw ain't got anything to give you, though."

"There's one thing."

"What's that?"

"That slingshot. It's keen, be nice to have."

Jock pulled the gitaway box over a rut on the road's shoulder. "I'll give it to you, an' maybe we can do somethin' extra, too."

"I think I know what I'd like to do. Do you think we'll be in Chattanooga by then?"

"I reckon. How come?"

"I've been looking at road signs, those big ones saying about a place called Rock City. I think I'd like to see it."

"I've been readin' them signs, too," Jock said. "Don't know what it's all about, but I tell you, me an' you'll go see for ourselves. An' maybe we can get ourselves one of them ice-cream cones. How's that for a birthday celebration?"

They got to the outer fringes of Chattanooga Friday evening. The fields were more open than they'd been farther back, and they had to take a dirt road and go two miles away from the highway before they found a stream and woods enough to camp in private. Saturday morning they were up early and had melted cheese on bread and hot coffee and four dried prunes each. They made it back to the highway and through the busy Saturday traffic of Chattanooga, Tennessee, and just after eleven o'clock they came to a huge white sign with a lighted-up black arrow pointing the way to Rock City.

"Wonder what it really is," Chris said.

"No way of knowin' till we get there," Jock said. "May be some kind of Indian place."

"Indian place?"

"Boy, Indians used to live all over this part of the country. Wasn't very civilized, but they made up for it by seein' the countryside."

"Do you think there's real Indians at Rock City?"

"We'll see soon 'nough."

They left the city street and turned at the marked route toward the winding road leading uphill. After half a block Jock stopped and looked ahead. All he could see was a hillside of trees and a narrow, disappearing black road. "Be a terrible place to get caught in the wintertime," he said.

The twisting, turning, bending, rising route they were on now was barely two cars wide along the infrequent straightaways, and not quite that at the turns. For the first hundred or so yards they kept to the side, but after the second sharp crook the dropoff was deep on the downside and sheer cliff on the upside. Jock finally gave up trying and guided the gitaway box onto the roadbed. One automobile crept up behind him, and another, and another, and they were forced to stay there because of the down-bound cars in the other lane. At the first long straight stretch, those three sped around, but at the next bend there was no new straightaway. This time three more cars, then four, then half a dozen, and finally Jock couldn't tell how many were strung out.

Chris looked back. "Paw-paw, those people want to get around us."

'Ain't keepin' 'em from it."

"But there's no room to pass."

"Road builders should of planned it for walkin' folks," Jock said. One of the drivers blew his horn and another chimed in. "Don't pay 'em any mind. Make like you don't hear 'em."

After a hundred or so yards, the operator of the third car got impatient and sped around the two others in front of him and cut in sharply, barely missing a car headed downhill in the opposite lane and making Jock hold up a step. "Trouble with folks, ain't got any patience. None at all."

Chris tried not to look behind but he looked once, anyway. The front-seat passenger of the first car motioned wildly for him and Jock to move out of the way. "That man doesn't like it."

"Ain't much I can do about it," Jock said.

They went another hundred yards and now the stream of cars must have stretched halfway back to the junction. The impatient man who'd waved once finally couldn't stand the wait any longer. He jumped out of the car while he trotted on ahead. "Old man, get that contraption off the road," he shouted. "Can't you see you're holding up a line of traffic?"

Jock stopped and looked at him. "Where you headed,

mister?"

"To Rock City. Where in the world else?"

"Me an' the boy's headed that way too. Reckon we'll have to stay on the road. Ain't no place else to go."

"But look at those cars you're holding up!"

"You standin' here jawin' ain't helpin' matters none," Jock said. "Just tag along, we'll make it." He began pulling once more.

The man stood there in the middle of the road, hands on hips, watching for a moment longer. Then he turned back to his car.

"Sure looks like you got a fine day for a birthday."

"Yes, sir. Paw-paw, are you going to stay in the middle of the road with all those cars back there?"

"Reckon we'll have to , 'less we come to a pullin'-off place."

Jock had no way of knowing how many cars were lined up behind him and the boy and the gitaway box by the time they reached the crest of the mountain and started down the slight incline toward the Rock City entrance. But however many there were, he and Chris did not have to pull into the parking lot; so they got to the steps and started toward the visitors' center before any car passengers did. On the wide landing in front of the building, Jock stopped and looked about at it and the three separate structures. "Don't see rock house number one, ain't nothin' here 'cept wood an' glass. Indians sure never lived in glass houses."

"Maybe you have to go through that long one first," Chris said.

"C'me on, boy, we'll see."

Chris held the door open while his grandfather tugged the box inside. Before them, glass counters and cases offered souvenir wares, an ashtray proclaiming *See Rock City,* American and Confederate flags, and a varied assortment of brassy-looking odds and ends that didn't seem to have any connection with Indians or whatever this place was all about. "Nothin' here," Jock said. "Ain't seen rock one or Indian one."

Chris pointed to a small booth off to the left. "That's the ticket window."

"Tickets for what?" Jock said.

"I guess for the city."

Jock tipped his hat to a man he'd bumped with the box and followed Chris across the floor. The sign was plain—two dollars for adults, one for children under twelve.

"Paw-paw, it's going to cost us three dollars to get in where it is."

"Three dollars!" Jock stopped and read the price sign carefully. "How many cities we come through, five, eight, maybe a dozen, an' it ain't cost us nothin' to get through none of 'em yet. Can't see just 'cause this'un's a-way on top of the mountain it's got to cost us. Trouble gettin' here an' all." He walked through the maze of counters to the glass wall beside the entrance door and looked out. "Boy, ain't nothin' out yonder 'cept a hillside full of rocks; don't see nothin' resemblin' a city."

"Maybe it's on the other side." Chris pressed his face against the glass. "Look, Paw-paw, there's a fish pool and a winding walk. And that over on the other side looks like a well."

"Reckon maybe it really *was* Indians up here," Jock said.

"Do you think they built the place?"

"Can't be for sure." Jock watched people going down the *out* path and coming back the *in* one. "Must be a sight, all them folks spendin' that kind of money to look." He turned back to the booth where the woman was collecting dollars and handing out little stubs. "Ma'am, what kind of place is that Rock City?"

"That's what it is," she said, "a city of rocks."

"Reckon it must be somethin' left over from when the Indians was all over the countryside. I 'member hearin' my pa tell how they was in a lot of places 'fore the turn of the century."

"Sir, I don't know that I understand what you mean, but the Indians had nothing to do with Rock City," the woman said.

"Must of been some hardy folks to climb the mountain an' build this place, then."

"Sir, nobody *built* Rock City. It's a formation—a rock formation right here on top of Lookout Mountain. And I might add, it's the most unusual thing of its kind east of the Mississippi River."

Jock looked out over the trees on the rolling mounds that hid the formation from where they were. "What you're tellin me is, the good Lord made it."

"Well, I guess you could say that," the woman said.

"An' you folks are just chargin' for seein' his

handiwork, that it?"

"Sir, I don't quite know what you're trying to get at, but the people who created this attraction went to a lot of trouble and expense so others could enjoy it. They cleaned out the loose rocks, built footbridges and walkways, they even built a swinging bridge."

"Done all that?" Jock said.

"They sure did. And all the way at the end, where the mountain drops straight down, they built a lookout point—you can stand out there and see seven states."

Jock wiped the back of his hand across his face and left his finger beside his nose to scratch away an itch. "Funny the good Lord didn't think of doin' that hisself. Reckon he must have been too busy figurin' out how to get up an' down the mountainside." He turned to Chris and took a step back from the window. "Come on, boy, many states as we seen an' many rocks as we slept behind, don't reckon there's nothin' out there worth spendin' three good dollars."

The woman looked at Chris. "There are the fairyland caverns. They're fascinating, particularly for children."

"Yes'm, I guess they must be, dependin' on what you got a taste for."

"Paw-paw, I'd like to see the caves and that place where you can look at seven states."

"Boy, soon's we get to Bucksville, I'll take you to see all kinds of caves. An' as for them states, less'n they got signs on 'em you can read from here, how'd a body know whether you was lookin' at Georgia, Tennessee, or Texas?"

"But it's my birthday and you said."

"Boy, I ain't goin' back on my word. I'm givin' you that slingshot. An' we aim to get that ice-cream cone. But, boy, we just ain't got any three dollars that don't get us nothin' but lookin'." He put his hand gently on Chris's shoulder and started guiding him toward the front. At the door he stopped once and looked back. "Day's gettin' hazy anyhow. Like as not you couldn't see no farther than the next hill."

Outside on the broad patio that extended almost all the way to the road, they worked the gitaway box around a woman trying to hold three children still long enough for a man to take a picture of them. Chris hesitated long enough to see the man trip the shutter then say, "Margaret Ann, I *told* you to stay still. Now look what you did," and to see the little curly haired child bury her head in the woman's lap and begin whimpering.

They had just sidestepped the photographer when a man across the way said, "Mister, wait up." Jock stopped and looked about. The tall, thin man coming toward them was dressed in light green trousers with little curlicues at the pockets and a wide belt and a matching light green shirt with beaded pockets and a wide tan hat and brown boots with high heels and stitching all about the tops. The woman with him was dressed similarly, except her clothes were light blue.

"Speakin' to me?" Jock said.

The man nodded. It wasn't quite what you'd call a smile, but the expression on his face showed traces of humor. "You're the fellow had traffic blocked coming up the mountain, weren't you?"

"Wasn't aimin' to block nobody," Jock said. "Folks that built that road didn't figure on walkers. Sorry to put you out."

"Oh, you didn't put us out. None at all. Me, I got a kick out of it, all those folks strung out like cows and not a thing in God's world they could do about it. Partner here, she climbed out and pulled herself a laurel sprig; she'll root it back home, thanks to you." The man squatted down and looked hard at the gitaway box. "This cart, never saw one like it."

"First'un I ever seen too," Jock said. "Built 'er myself. Me an' the boy needed it for travelin'."

"Like a trailer?"

"The pullin' kind," Jock said.

The man looked up at him. "Mind if we take a picture of it?"

"Not at all. Boy, back outa the man's way."

"No," the man said, "you and the boy, too."

They stood still behind the box while the man backed off and took three pictures. Jock stood stiff and straight and looked directly into the camera. Chris raised one shoulder and lowered the other and put his right hand on the gitaway box; he didn't know what to do with his left so he held it nervously behind him. "Thanks." The man looked at his wife. "Partner," he said, "Jeffry'd like one of those." He looked back at Jock. "That's my grandboy. He's eight going on nine, always pulling some kind of wagon around the place. One of those cut down to size'd sure please 'im. Say you made it?"

Jock nodded.

"What's on the inside?"

"Me an' the boy's b'longin's." Jock opened the side.

"Will you look at that?" The man crouched, studying the partitions. "Cubbyholes and everything, I never seen the match of it. What do you think, partner?"

The woman nodded. Her manner was gentle and easy, and though she didn't smile, her expression was soft. "Maybe you could have one made for him, that is, if this gentleman doesn't mind."

"No'm," Jock said. "Ain't nothin' to it, you take a hunk of plywood an' cut two sides about three foot long an' two foot high an'—"

"Wait a minute," the man interrupted. "How much would you charge me to make a sketch of it—draw it like you'd make it?"

Jock thought of the cost for Chris to go in and see Rock City and he was about to say a dollar when he remembered the ice-cream cones. "Come to a buck an' two-bits."

"A dollar and a quarter, that's a strange price."

"Well, that's my fee."

"You sure that's enough?" the man asked.

Jock looked at Chris and he remembered what the woman had said about the rocks. "I tell you what, mister, you pay the boy's fare to see them rocks an' let him tag along with you—me, I ain't goin', seen enough rocks when I was a kid—an' let me have some paper an' a pencil, an' I'll have it drawed up when you come back, measurin's an' all."

"A deal," the man said. He went inside the souvenir shop and returned with a tablet of unlined paper and two pencils.

Jock took them and dug the broken half of a carpenter's rule from the gitaway box. "Boy, you stick close to them folks, but don't go givin' 'em any trouble, you hear."

"I hear." The happy birthday look was on Chris's face when he took the man's hand.

Forty-five minutes later they came again from the souvenir shop and there was an almost laugh on the boy's face. "A fine youngster you have here," the man said.

Jock nodded. "Like his pa."

The man's own expression eased into a look of genuine interest. "He told me about his family."

Jock looked at Chris, then back at the man. "Terrible thing, but he oughtn' of said nothin'; us Ransomes don't talk of our troubles."

"I'm sorry, but I didn't know so I asked. No harm meant."

"No harm done."

Jock folded the sheets of paper he'd made the sketches on. Then remembering that he had not pointed out the scale he used, he opened them and held them out. "Done it three inches to the foot. Reckon whoever you get to make it can go by these lines."

The man glanced at the carefully drawn pieces with the crude arrows showing how they fitted together. "With that and the picture I made to go by, I think I could do it myself." He refolded them and handed them to his wife. "Long journey you and the boy have to make."

"Ain't as long as it was from up yonder. Done come most of it."

"The boy told me, and all I can say is you've got guts."

"Nothin' special." Jock closed the side of the gitaway box. "Two bits an' me an' you are even. An' I'm much obliged for you takin' the boy along. You had a good time, didn't you, boy?"

Chris nodded. "I wish you could have seen it, Paw-paw, all those big rocks and that tunnel and those rooms where the little dolls were, like a fairy land."

Jock couldn't help smiling. "Reckon by the time you get done tellin' me what you seen it'll be like I was right there alongside." He looked off down the hill. "Time me an' you was movin' on."

"Mr. Ransome,"the man said.

Jock turned back to him. "Yes, sir?"

The man put his hand in his pocket and took it out and put it back a second time. He took it out a second time. "I hope you and the boy have a successful trip."

Jock saw the motion and read it. "Yes, sir, an' I'm much obliged again for you not doin' what you was of a mind to do. We'll make it."

"I'm sure you will, but one thing before you go," and this time he put his right hand in his right pocket. "The boy tells me this is his birthday."

"That's right."

"I hope you won't take offense if I give him a little something," the man said. Jock wasn't sure. "Just a little token." The man palmed from his pocket a small bone-handled knife with two blades and a bottle opener and a screwdriver. "I bought it for Jeffrey, and Partner, here, she didn't know I did it and she bought one exactly like it. The kid can't use both."

Jock saw the expression on Chris's face. From his own pocket he took out the snap-to purse and fished a penny from it. "Reckon it'd please him." He handed the penny to Chris. "But, boy," he said, "you give this here to the man for it. You take a knife without givin' nothin' in turn, you cut off a friend." He glanced at the man. "An' you sure wouldn't want to cut off this friend."

The man smiled and took the penny.

Chris took the knife and fondled it and opened all the blades and closed them again and fondled it once more.

"What do you say, boy?"

"Thank you. I sure do thank you, mister."

"You're welcome. Just be careful and don't cut yourself."

"He'll take care," Jock said.

"Good luck."

"An' the same to you."

They were working the gitaway box down the flagstone steps when Jock heard the man say to the woman he called Partner, "A shame there's too few of his kind left in this old world."

"Paw-paw, it's a fine birthday," Chris said.

As they started down the road Jock almost stepped on a wide red and white cardboad See Rock City bumper tag like they'd seen on cars in the parking lot. He picked it up and hooked it across the back of the gitaway box. "That's to show we done something special on the day, too."

12 ....

They made it only a few miles out of Chattanooga that afternoon. When they came to a railroad overpass crossing route 11, Jock decided it was time to stop for the evening. They left the highway and worked their way around a thickly wooded hillock, letting it act as a buffer against traffic noise. Their sleep was restless that night, however, because of the trains. Won't never stop near no track beds again, Jock decided.

They walked all day Sunday and by late afternoon on Monday, after crossing through a barren northwest corner of the state of Georgia and making it past the state line into Alabama, they reached a point where the road arrows pointed two ways to Birmingham. Jock guided the gitaway box off the shoulder and beyond a drainage ditch to the uncertain shade of a huge twisted pine tree.

"Is this where we're camping tonight?" Chris asked.

"This ain't no place to stop, boy. This here's a kind of fork an' we got to figure which way's the best'un."

"Do they both get us to the same place?"

"If the road sign's right, they do."

"Maybe it doesn't matter which one we go on."

"Common sense says one of 'em is shorter 'an the other'n goes through a heap of towns. Never figured road builders was the smartest folks in the world, but they're dumber'n me an' you put together if they run two big highways side by side an' the two of 'em goin' to the same places."

He dug the map out of the gitaway box and spread it across his knees. He took the stub of a pencil from his coat pocket and licked the point. "Right here's where I think we done got to, an' this here's the road to our left an' that other'n's the one to the right."

Chris stopped whittling on the piece of pine bark and leaned over his grandfather's shoulder. "Can't tell which is which."

"That'un yonder, that's the new one, an' the way it looks on this here map, it don't go through nothin' but country."

"If we went that way we wouldn't have all those city people looking at us."

"Trouble is, a new road an' all, wouldn' likely be no stores along the way, an' it seems a long way from here to there."

Chris stared at the litle numbers. "Near as I can tell, looks like ninety-three or ninety-five or ninety-seven. That's a lot of miles, Paw-paw."

"We come a heap farther. You know, boy, we ain't more'n a hundred an' fifty miles from Bucksville."

"We've come that far," Chris said.

"An' walkin' most of it." Jock looked at the boy. "We take the old road. Like as not we can get some work down the way, might even work us up enough to ride the bus on from there."

Chris sat down and began whittling again. "Paw-paw, maybe we ought not to hurry. Maybe when we get there Aunt Jessie won't have anyplace for us and we'll have to go back."

"Boy, hush that kind of talk. Sure she'll have a place for us, somethin' to make do with for a spell, anyhow."

"All the same, it'd be all right if we don't hurry."

Jock made his own interpretation of the uncertain words and the certain look of doubt on the boy's face. "Maybe you want to camp along the way so's you can shoot that slingshot."

"You could teach me how to use it."

So they picked the newer interstate route that sliced through farms and countrysides, bypassing the towns and sidestepping the wide-place-in-the-road villages. Before moving out on it, however, they turned back to the little store at the intersection and Jock spent $3.81 of the $5.00 he had left for the one-shot-sized cans of hash and peas and spaghetti and pork with beans. He decided against eggs, what with the heat and all, and he skipped the bacon, too, because the price was too high, but he did buy a half-pound slice of fat back and had it double wrapped in waxed paper so its grease wouldn't drop down on the other articles in the gitaway box. And he got a box of pancake mix that required only water. Finally, he bought a box of dried apples and one of prunes, and he chose half a dozen powder mixes for grape, orange, and cherry drinks. At the filling station across from the store, he filled the three empty peanut-butter jars with water. "Never can tell, mightn' come on a crick or spring when we most need it."

The gitaway box was fully loaded and heavier than it had been during the first part of the trip. They couldn't pull it quite as fast with all the extra weight, and besides, the little rubber tires were worn nearly down to the metal rims. When they took to the gravel shoulder of the interstate highway, they slipped a long sturdy stick through the handle so they could pull together. That afternoon they made only four miles before Chris said he was tired and hungry and thirsty. At the first little stream they came to, they pushed their way through the weedy underbrush to the shade of a towering oak and made camp. That night it was too hot for a fire so they ate cold pork and beans and crackers and washed them down with cherry-flavored water.

Tuesday and Wednesday were hot, and Thursday was even hotter. And unlike some of the roads they'd traveled, the interstate did not have any overhanging trees to shade away the sun, not even for a moment.

They had, then, to pace themselves—walking for fifty-five minutes by Jock's old Waltham pocket watch and stopping for five and taking one swallow of water. Friday came up cloudy and drizzling, and heavy dampness hung all about them.

"Reckon a few drops of rain ain't goin' to hurt us none," Jock said. "Beats the sun scorchin' your scalp."

"Don't mind it in the daytime," the boy said. "Just so it don't rain t'night."

But it did rain that night—not hard, just enough to make everything soggy so the fire kept going out and the coffee water couldn't get hot enough to provide more than tan liquid. They hunted till they found some overhanging rocks with thick vines drooping down, and they pushed the blanket roll as far into the crevasse as they could and huddled inside its meager protection. Neither slept well.

"Paw-paw, maybe we ought to cross over to that other road; might find an old barn or boxcar to sleep in."

"Wouldn't know which way to get there." Jock patted the boy on the shoulder. "Never mind, we'll make it."

But late Sunday evening, after six and one-half days on the interstate highway, with no working interruptions or short-haul rides, and with nothing to break the monotony of the open land except an occasional farm in the distance and the infrequent but ceaseless whizzing by of cars and trucks, Jock knew he wasn't going to make it. In the little box he had tried to keep hidden from Chris, there was one pill left, and the tightness in his chest had nagged him for two days. That evening when they stopped, he had rubbed his arm hard, crudely rousing circulation. They worked their way back from the roadside along the bank of the widest stream they'd come to. Jock couldn't be sure whether it was a big creek or a little river. At a point where it appeared that once a small herd of cows had pressed the grass and weeds down around a thicket of crab apple and persimmon trees, they stopped.

"Boy, how long since you had a good washin'?"

"I forget," Chris said, "but it was three days ago I think."

"Ain't goin' to find a better washin' hole than this'un," Jock said.

"Looks big enough to swim in."

"You go ahead. Paw-paw's wore out."

"Aren't you going to go in?"

"D'rectly. But boy, you git in an' swim some 'fore dark."

They ate warmed-up hash spread over four crackers laid out in squares on the pie tins and chewed for a while on four dried prunes each. And they washed them down with good hot coffee, because this time the fire was hot and there was plenty of water to make it. Then Chris got up without being told and went down to the stream to wash the utensils. When he returned, again without prompting, he took out the blanket and laid it over a spread-out pile of long brown grass.

Jock watched him carefully, observing the sure way he moved and seeing the ready contrast between Chris now and the Chris of four weeks earlier. The hurt was still in him. Jock had seen the strained look in his eyes when something reminded him of Stella or Andy, and he had sensed at times the tightness of near-tears just before sleep. But the sun of boy in him was burning through the cloud of fear, and he was beginning to warm to their life together.

Jock did not like the idea of having to tell him now, with their traveling nearly done, that the pace and mode of the journey would have to change.

"Paw-paw, how much longer is it?"

"Not long, not more'n thirty-five or forty miles; be there 'fore you know it."

The boy put away the pan and the pie tins and the coffeepot and closed the gitaway box. "Is that medicine you take going to last?"

Jock could have asked what medicine, but he'd shown the boy truth, taught him truth during all the time they'd been on the road, and now was no time to hide. "Fact is, I got one more pill, boy."

"Maybe we better get some more in the next town."

"Good idea."

He spoke true, but not the full truth. And that night after Chris had gone to sleep Jock lay on his back, mouth open, breathing deep, and looking straight up through the tree branches into the starry hills of heaven. For him, he knew there would be no walking on, not from here, not tomorrow. The heavy ache and then the numbness had crept into his legs, and the weight of all the miles they'd walked pressed down upon him. He touched the child gently, then lay still.

When morning came Jock got up from the blanket and walked over to the trunk of the big sycamore and sat down again. Two days' rest and two more pills and he could make it. He had neither and would have neither if they remained here. He let Chris gather twigs and limbs and build the fire, watched as the boy put water and coffee grounds together and place the pot on the fire just so. Then he showed him how to mix pancake flour and water to make a thick batter and how to hold the little skillet over the flame. When Chris had made four such cakes, skillet-bottom big and stiff as cornbread, Jock showed him how to pour boiling water over dried prunes for thin syrup. Then as they sat side by side on the ground eating, Jock nodded. "Done well, boy. Paw-paw couldn' of done no better hisself."

Once again he let the boy wash the items they'd used, but at packing-away time, he stopped him. "No use to put 'em back."

"We're going to stay here another day?"

Jock looked straight into his face. "Come here, boy, sit down by me." Chris came closer and squatted down and waited. "Boy, Paw-paw's done travelin', just can't walk no more. Now—wait a minute, 'fore you go askin' questions, you lissen to me. You lissen real good, you hear? We ain't more'n three, maybe four mile from Bardock City. That's where this here road an' the old'un come together. You got to walk there, you hear, all by yourself you got to walk there. Now, now, just you lissen a minute. Ain't no other way, you hear; you go there an' you hitchhike you a ride to Bucksville, that's all the way through Birmin'ham an' some past Bessemer. You remember Bessemer, don't you? It's where we used to buy shoes an' things."

Jock stopped and took a deep breath and stretched out his leg to ease the cramp he was getting. "If you ain't sure how to get to your Aunt Jessie's place, stop in Willie Timmons's store an' ask Willie the way. Tell 'im who you are, 'cause you done growed up so he wouldn' know you. An' you tell Aunt Jessie an' them to get in that ol' car they got an' come after me. I ain't goin no place; I'll be right here waitin'."

"Paw-paw, I'd be scared to do all that."

"Boy, you got no call to be skeered. Anybody run off a whiskeyed-up bully like you done a way back, kept step to step with me all the way to here, wouldn' be nothin' to go the balance on your own."

The boy looked straight into his face. "Paw-paw, are you going to die? I don't want you to die."

Jock's hand shook as he put it on the boy's arm. He made his mouth shape a smile. "Ain't about to, much as me an' you got to git done, now ain't no time for me to go dyin'. Now, you git on. An' boy," he said, "take this here slip of paper the doctor give me. Tell Aunt Jessie she better get me some of them pills like I been takin'." He handed Chris the crumpled copy of the prescription. "An' you best take Paw-paw's watch so you'll know how far back from Bardock City to come lookin'."

Chris slowly took the watch and stared at its face. "A watch won't tell how far anything is."

"Take a little figurin'," Jock said. "Me an' you been

walkin' 'bout a mile ever' twenty-five minutes, take you an' hour an' a half to get to Bardock City, that'll be most four mile. Now, you go over to the stream an' wet your hair down. Ain't nobody'll give you a ride lookin' like a tramp."

The big watch said ten minutes after eight when Chris started away from the camping spot. Just beyond the edge of its clearing, however, he stopped and ran back and threw his arms around Jock's neck. "Paw-paw, I don't want to go. Maybe I can stop somebody on the road; maybe they'll come help."

Jock patted his back. "Boy, we ain't asked for help yet, an' we don't aim to. Anybody give you a ride, you get the name an' add-ress; tell 'em I'll send 'em the fare soon's I can."

This time Chris kept going when he reached the wooded path. At the side of the road he stopped and turned around and looked back through the underbrush, but he couldn't see Jock. He wiped the back of his hand across his face and started walking southwest. When he came to the slight rise in the roadway, he stopped again and looked back once more. The countryside was still, and now the stream was out of sight.

He had no way of knowing how far he'd walked when he took the watch from his pocket and stared at the hands. Ten minutes, that's all the time he'd been walking, just ten minutes. He put it away. "Please don't die, Paw-paw," he said out loud.

One hour and twenty-seven minutes later he came to the huge white sign that read Bardock City in big letters and population 5,625 in smaller ones. This highway was narrower that the interstate they'd been following, and there were many more trucks. Most of them slowed down when they came to the sign, and it looked like a solid stream of traffic going through the town.

With the uncertainty of a firster, he raised his right hand and stuck out his thumb toward one of the trucks, then toward the next three cars. They went by with no sign of seeing him. He let the next five go by, trying to look for some kind of clue as to which to flag at. He wiped his hand across his hair, remembering what Jock had said. He stood straight and when the next truck came along he raised the thumb once again. The driver stopped thirty yards down the road and Chris ran toward it. The man in the cab leaned toward the window.

"Where you goin', boy?"

"Bucksville."

"Bucksville, never heered of it. Reckon you better try the next'un." He drove off and left the boy standing there.

Chris looked across the street and saw that the man at the corner filling station was watching him. He fidgeted with his belt and adjusted the front of his shirt. And while he was making up his mind whether to try from that spot or walk down to the next corner, he saw a boy running a power lawn mower on the wide lot beside a new brick building. "I won't do it," he said. "I won't go on to Bucksville without Paw-paw."

He did not know why he said it. All he was certain of when the words came out was a sudden welling up inside him of one clear resolve.

He did a half a turn about and studied the hodgepodge signs that hung out at the building fronts. There was one saying Drug Store and one half a block away that said Bus Terminal. Didn't seem quite proper, a place no bigger than Bardock City with a sign saying terminal, but there it was. Chris stepped back from the edge of the road and over the curbing and onto the narrow, cracked sidewalk. Without hurrying, he didn't want to call attention to himself, he walked down toward the signs. At the drugstore he went inside, all the way back to the high counter where the druggist was pouring a brown liquid into a tight-necked bottle. When he finshed, he glanced at Chris. "Can I help you, son?"

Chris held out the prescription. "My grandfather needs this."

The man took the paper and smoothed out the creases. "Let's see now, these come in two sizes, a dozen and fifty, which one?"

"What's the cost of the dozen?"

"Dozen's a dollar, fifty's three dollars, better buy the fifty, cheaper."

Chris didn't have a penny in his pocket. "The dollar size, that's the one he said to get. I'll come back later to pick them up."

"Be ready in thirty minutes," the man said.

From the drugstore, Chris went down the short distance to the bus terminal, discovering when he got there that it used to be a filling station with the pumps gone and only the covered-over drive as a reminder. He pulled open the rickety screen door and went to the ticket window. "Mister, how much is it to Bucksville?"

"Bucksville—Bucksville. The bus don't go all the way, have to get off at Bessemer."

"How much is it for a grown-up?"

"Man or boy, it's still eighty cents," the man said.

"Thank you, and I'll be back."

When Chris got to the street again, he stood on the corner, gazing vaguely one direction then the other. He was beginning to head toward the residential part when he caught a glimpse of a faded blue and white sign with the word Taxi in fresh black letters across it. At the curb nearby an equally faded blue and white car sat, motor idling and the driver leaning back with his hat pulled down to hide his eyes. Chris started reluctantly toward it, stopped and decided against the idea, then finally crossed over. He went to the passenger side and leaned through the open window. "Mister, what do you charge for taking people?"

The man lifted his hat long enough to see the boy, then let it fall back. "How far's up, kid?"

"What I mean is, do you go by the mile or what?"

"D'pends," the man said. "Short haul, it's by the mile. A trip, say, to Birmin'ham or more, it'd be a hard price." He glanced from under the hat brim at Chris.

"What's the price by the mile?" Chris said. His words came slow and unsteady.

"Forty-five cents for the first'un, thirty a mile from then on. You want to go somewhere, kid, an' you got the money, call me, you hear."

"Yes, sir, thank you, sir." He backed away slowly, adding up miles and mile costs. Let's see, forty-five cents for the first mile, that would leave seven to go, seven times thirty, that came to $2.10, and add the forty-five to it, the total ran to $2.55.

He crossed back and walked down to the nearest corner. Stopping to be sure he was headed toward where the houses were, he then moved along the even more cracked-up sidewalk till he came to a square of plain hard dirt without a blade of grass. He got down on his knees and used a stubby twig to scratch the figures out: $1.00 for medicine, $1.60 for bus tickets, $2.55 for the taxi man. Underneath the figures he scratched out a line and added carefully—five and zero and zero makes five, five and six and zero are eleven, one down and carry one, one and one and one and two are five—altogether, $5.15. That was the amount needed, $5.15. Except for the time last winter before Christmas when he had saved from his allowance to buy Mommy that flower vase she'd set her heart on, he'd never before put together that much.

He was going to do it today.

He stood up and brushed the dirt from his wrinkled jeans and started toward the houses again. Across the second street, he stopped at a corner and stared at the fronts of three of them, studying their lawns. Huge trees covered the yard of one, and the thin grass seemed to be struggling just to remain alive. Next door, the thick green carpet was even and closely cropped, as if a mower had been run over it just the day before. The third yard looked scraggly and he concentrated on the front door of the house. Uncertainly, he headed for it.

After his third knock, he heard shuffling steps across a bare floor and a woman came to the screen. Though it was midmorning, she looked like she was still wearing a nightgown and her hair was all done up in curlers. Cradled against her hip was a young baby with a teething ring in its mouth. "Yeah, what d'you want, kid?" she said.

Chris shuffled one foot. "You wouldn't want to get your grass cut, would you?"

She stared at him from the tousled hair down to the scuffed-up shoes. "Kid, you ain't big enough to cut nobody's yard. The ol' man does it when he ain't off rattin' around, anyhow."

"It wouldn't cost you much."

"I said no, and don't come botherin' me again. Can't you see I got too much to do? Besides, the ol' man don't want just anybody messin' with his mower."

Chris walked down the steps and out to the sidewalk. He stopped there a moment and thought back to the road and the hitchhiking. He touched his tongue to his lips and hesitated, then he turned down the block.

The woman at the fourth house he came to wasn't like the others. Chris couldn't help thinking of that Mrs. Ringles back in Bristol, the way she moved and the quick way she talked. "Son, do you think you're big enough to run a power mower?"

"Yes ma'am, I learned how last summer."

"And you know how to keep your feet away from the

blades?"

"Yes, ma'am."

She came out on the porch and carefully looked him over. After a minute she made up her mind. "The mower's in the shed out back, and there's a can of gas. Put some in but don't let it run over, you understand?"

"Yes, ma'am." He turned about and was starting toward the shed.

"Son, how much do you charge?"

"Well." He looked out at the grass, not knowing what figure to name.

"Did you ever cut for pay before?"

Chris remembered Jock. "No, ma'am."

"Thought as much." Her light smile was sort of friendly. "The last young fellow did it for a dollar and a half," she said. "You do it right and I'll pay you the same."

"Yes, ma'am."

An hour and forty-five minutes later he put the mower away and wiped the dirt off his hands onto his trousers. The woman came out and looked over the yard. "You did even better than the last boy." She nodded and handed him a dollar bill, then counted out three quarters.

Chris held the money in his palm a moment, staring at it. Slowly but firmly he took the third quarter and handed it back to her. "Ma'am, my grandfather says a bargain's a bargain, and we fixed on a dollar and a half."

The woman stared at the money and at him and at the money again.

"Boy, I never heard of anybody turning money down.

Your grandfather, whoever he is, you tell him never mind where you came from and never mind where you're going, you'll get there." She glanced at the short sidewalk running from the front of the porch to the street. "You sweep that off for the quarter, how about that?"

"Yes, ma'am."

That accounted for the first dollar, seventy-five.

From there he knocked on the doors of seven other houses before he got another job. It was always the same thing—boy, you're not big enough to run a power mower; or boy, my husband cuts the grass when he's home; or boy, my son cuts for me and the neighbors around here.

But at the seventh, an old man came in answer to his knock, one foot in a cast and hobbling with a cane. He frowned like frowning was the only way he knew how to make his face look. "Don't reckon you c'n do a decent job. Ain't seen a kid yet knowed how to work; all they ever want's the money an' never a care f'r doin' nothin' right."

"Yes, sir, mister, but I'll bargain with you."

"Bargain with me?"

"Yes, sir. I'll cut it and you look at it. If you don't like the way I do, you don't pay me."

The frown halfway broke. "You think I'll get soft, huh, an' pay you anyhow."

"No, sir, my grandfather says if a job's worth doing, it's worth doing right and that's what I'll do. I'll do it right."

"An' how much d'you want f'r doin' it right?"

The yard was larger than the one he'd gotten a dollar and a half for. "Would two dollars be too much?"

"It would, one-fifty's all I'll pay, all I give the last'un. An' you better do it good or you won't get that."

It took Chris two hours and fifteen minutes to cut the lawn, and he was hungrier than he ever remembered being when he finished. He rolled the mower back under the house where the man kept it and knocked on the back door. The old man came out and spoke not a word while he walked all over the yard. He slowly circled each of the giant oak trees and he poked his cane beneath the heavy shrubbery to be sure the boy had gotten up close. His frown did not disappear when he completed his inspection. "Good thing you didn' tear up none o' them shrubs," he said. Very carefully he fished a worn dollar bill from one pocket, then counted out three dimes and four nickels and handed them to Chris. "Don't look to me f'r no praise. You done no more'n you bargained for."

Chris thanked him and walked down the narrow drive and to the street once more. Out of sight of the man and his house, and beyond the tree shade, he took out the money and counted it all. Three twenty-five. He scratched his head and figured. Take that from the five fifteen and he needed another two dollars. But right now he had to eat.

Back at the main street of the little town, he wandered out the way he'd come to the battered and beaten little cafe stuck onto the side of the old bus-terminal filling station. He went in and sat on the edge of the counter stool farthest back.

A round-faced, sweaty-browed waitress came up to him and said, "What'll it be, sonny?"

He looked at the signs tacked unevenly on the wall. "A hot dog and a glass of milk," he said, "and maybe a piece of pie."

"*Maybe* a piece of pie?"

"How much is it?"

"Fifteen cents."

"I guess not, then. Just the hot dog and milk."

It took her ten minutes to get them for him and he needed only five to eat. "How much?"

"Twenty-five and twelve and one cent tax'll be thirty-eight cents."

"And can I have a nickel bar of candy?"

She pulled a chocolate bar from the box beside the cash register. "Forty-three, oughta be another penny for tax but I ain't going to charge you."

He handed her two quarters and she gave him back the change. "Must be new around here, ain't you?" she said. "Never seen you before."

"Yes'm." He went out before she could ask anything more.

And now he had only $2.82. He chewed on the candy bar as he turned the opposite direction from where he'd been making the rounds.

It was after two o'clock when he started on the second effort. It was after four before he came to the huge house and large shaded yard where a woman was bending over and chopping at the dirt with a small-handled hoe. Chris waited to see what she was doing, then crossed the lawn to where she was. "Ma'am?"

She started and glanced about. "Oh, you gave me a fright," she said.

"Didn't mean to, ma'am, but I was wondering if you need any help."

"You mean digging?"

"Digging, cutting grass, anything."

She looked him over much as did the first woman he'd seen earlier. "You don't look to be big enough for digging." Her voice was even and gentle, with just a fringe of friendliness.

"Yes, ma'am, I can. I helped my grandfather dig a big ditch just last week."

She studied his browned arms and dirty fingers, the firm, sure way he stood there watching her. "Well, I've these six bushes to plant. You can try, and I'll pay you twenty-five cents a hole."

Chris looked at the little hoe, then he stooped over and picked up the curved spade. "I can do better with this."

An hour and a few minutes later they had all the holes dug and the shrubbery in. Chris carefully pulled the dirt up to the roots while the woman mixed in powdered fertilizer and poured water from a kitchen pot.

"Somebody's certainly taught you garden care," she said.

"My grandfather, he can do 'most anything. I stay with him," he said before she could ask any questions.

When they finished, he took the hose and sprayed the

mud and dirt from his hands, then wiped them dry on his trousers. She brought the money out to him—a dollar bill and two quarters. "Young man, if you can come back next Saturday I might have more planting to do. You work well."

"Thank you, ma'am, but I guess we won't be here then."

"Oh."

"Yes, ma'am, I think we'll be moving."

From there he walked up toward the next corner, not realizing till he got almost there that he was now retracing his steps back to where he had started that morning. He was just passing the house where the woman with the baby slung on her hips had told him she didn't need any help because her old man did the lawn work when he saw her standing out in the yard looking up at the lower branches of a huge tree. She now wore gray shorts and a white shirt, but her hair was still rolled up in those curler things. She heard him passing by and motioned to him. "Little boy, you want to make some money. I'll give you a dime to get my cat out of the tree."

He peered through the thick leaves and saw the white kitten crouched way out on a heavy limb, tail swishing back and forth, a little mewing sound coming from it. Ordinarily, he'd welcome the chance to climb a tree like that; it was bigger than those back where he'd been, and he'd have liked the contest with the cat. But he couldn't forget the way she had spoken to him.

"Ma'am, I get half a dollar for rescuing cats."

She turned full around and put her hand on her hip.

"Half a dollar! Half a dollar my eye. I never, I just never." She looked up into the tree once more. "Dumb cat, just stay there."

Chris shuffled toward the corner. When he heard a door slam shut he glanced around. The woman was gone. Quickly he went back to the tree, keeping its trunk between himself and the front of the house, and shinnied up. With all the skill of a little boy in a big friendly oak, he worked his way out to the kitten. Carefully he reached out and wrapped his fingers under it, saying "nice kitty, nice kitty, nice kitty." When he caught it he leaned down and dropped it onto a thick patch of grass. The cat hunched down, stunned for the moment, then ran high tail and arch back toward the sanctuary of the porch. Chris watched for a moment, then twisted over the limb, deftly caught at it and let himself to the ground. "You can keep your old dime," he said aloud to no one.

From that corner he walked three blocks over, toward an area of houses he hadn't been in, and once more began knocking on doors. It was dusk by the time he got his fifth "no we don't need the grass cut." At the sixth house he was too tired to bound up the steps and he was almost certain of the answer he would get. He went anyway. At his knock a huge man came to the door, a can of beer in one hand. "Yeah, sonny-boy, what d'you want?"

"Would you like your grass cut?" Chris said.

The man stared down at him, then started laughing. "Grass cut, grass cut. Hey, Sue, come out an' lookit what wants to cut the grass."

A woman came from the indoor shadows and stared, too. "Little tramp, more'n likely he don't want to cut grass. More'n likely he wants to see what he can steal."

The man laughed again, then the laughter died suddenly. "Boy, you better git, you hear? Tell your folks we don't cater to your kind. Wouldn't let the likes o' you touch my mower, anyhow."

Chris turned away and went slowly down the steps and out to the sidewalk. Dusk was spilling over into darkness, and even while he wished he could find one more yard to cut, he knew he could not see to run the mower. One more, just one more, just a dollar and some, that's all. But the dark beat him to it.

He headed uncertainly back the way he'd come in town that morning, chewing his lip. Too late now to catch a ride, too late to get to Aunt Jessie's, too late to do anything but go back and look for Paw-paw.

Thing was, when he reached the edge of town, it was even too late and dark to do that. Maybe he could find his way in the daytime, but not now, not now and he knew it. At the fork he stopped and looked out the highway, then back toward town. He swallowed and bit back the taste of doubt. The choice of what to do was no longer his.

With slow and unwilling steps he made his way back to the dingy cafe where he had bought the hot dog and milk. This time he ordered a hamburger and milk. "And one of those pieces of apple pie, and put it in a sack for me, please ma'am."

This waitress was tall and thin and black-haired, and

she didn't ask any questions. "Fifty-seven cents," she said. He counted out the coins and gave her even money.

On the darkened walk once more, he returned toward the fork in the road, to a high billboard sign he'd seen earlier, with dark green lattice filling in the gap between the sign and the ground. He waited till no cars were coming, then he worked his way behind it, into the shadows. He pressed down the tall, thick grass that had not been cut. He squatted and sat, and sprawled out and ate. And before he could swallow the last of the milk, child tiredness came over him. He stretched out and closed his eyes. Then he wadded the paper sack the food came in and made a pillow of it. He sobbed once and drew his arms tight about him, and he went to sleep.

A truck backfired during the night and Chris stirred. A car squealed its brakes during the early hours of the morning and he turned on his side, and the sun came up hard and hot against the back of the billboard and he woke.

He got up and stole around the side, making sure no one saw him, then crossed over and went down a block to the first filling station. In the men's room he dowsed water on his face and hair, relieved himself, and went outside. "Hey, kid, that's for customers," the man in the gray overalls said.

"Yes, sir," Chris said. "Maybe I can buy some gas someday." The station's clock said seven-thirty and so did Paw-paw's watch.

At the cafe for the third time, he bought an egg

sandwich and a cup of coffee. "Mighty young to be drinkin' that stuff," the waitress said. She was the same one who'd sold him the lunch the day before, but she didn't seem to remember. "That'll be forty-three cents." He paid and ate quickly.

It was not yet eight when he left the main street and turned toward the residential area. This time he chose the houses on the other side of town, away from where he'd been on Monday. He walked three blocks before he came to a section with yards that looked like somebody cared. The first was neatly trimmed, with the fresh-green cuttings still on the surface, as if the mowing had been done earlier that same morning. The second was equally smooth, though the browner clippings looked like a two-day earlier job.

At the third house, a man was unfastening the tailgate of a pickup truck, parked at the end of the driveway. Chris looked at the yard, then went toward the man. "Mister, I can cut your grass for you."

The man looked at him. "Don't need it t'day, got too much else to see to. You didn't see a fella who looked like he was huntin' someplace, did you?"

"No, sir."

"That's the trouble. People say they're comin' to work, swear on a stack o' Bibles a mile high they'll be there by seven, but it's the last you hear of 'em."

"If you got some work, maybe I could do it."

"Naw, boy, this here's man's work. Got a whole truckbed full o' two-by-four studs, rough'uns. Fifty of 'em I got to get toted over yonder." He pointed to the foundation of a new building at the back of his house.

Chris walked to the tailgate and put a hand on one of the pieces of lumber. "I could carry these, mister."

"One, yeah—four or five, maybe," the man said, "but not all of 'em. Boy, that's fifty you're lookin' at."

Chris lifted the end of one two-by-four. "I could try, mister. You could let me try."

The man frowned and studied Chris's arms. "Must be stronger'n you look, wantin' to do that."

"Please, mister, let me try," Chris pleaded.

The man stared for a minute longer and sighed. "All right. All right, boy, you try. For every ten you tote, I'll give you half a buck. You tote 'em all, I'll pay you three dollars. Three whole dollars."

Chris grabbed one and hurried across the yard with it. He took a second, hurrying with it, too, and a third.

"Boy, you'll run plumb outa gas goin' at it so. I got to mix this here concrete; you just take your time, ain't no rush."

Chris moved a bit slower on the next two, then he fixed on a given pace—pick up a stud, carry it so many steps, put it down and pause, go back to the truck and pause, pick up the next and go with it. And on and on.

An hour later, by the time his count reached twenty-five, his legs were shaky. At the fortieth, his feet were hurting and he had splinters in a finger and a thumb. He tripped with the forty-eighth, but he got right up and carried it to the stack. Very carefully he put it in place. He took extra time with the forty-ninth. And when he finally put the fiftieth with the rest, he sat down heavily. He breathed hard and picked at the splinters. "Mister," and he had a hard time getting the words out, he was that worn and weary, "that's all of them—right down to the last one."

The man came over to the pile, wiping the cement mixture from his hand onto his pants. He looked from the stack to the empty truckbed and back. "Kid, I'd of never b'lieved it, no bigger'n you are. You sure must want somethin' mighty bad to struggle the way you done."

"Yes, sir, I do," Chris said.

The man took a battered billfold from his pocket and handed the boy three wrinkled ones. "You come back Saturday," he said. "A kid wants to work that hard, I'll let you cut the grass."

Chris thanked the man but he made no comment about cutting the grass. "I sure would like a drink of water."

The man pointed to the hydrant. "Help yourself."

Chris swallowed four mouthfuls, then dashed water on his face.

He stood up and wiped his hands across his shirt. "So long, mister."

He walked back across the yard and out to the street. He went slowly to the corner and around it, till he was out of the man's sight. He took all the money from his pocket and counted it: *$6.32!*

He started toward the main street again. First he moved slowly, stretching the muscles of his legs. Then he began trotting. Then he began running. He ran down the cracked and broken sidewalk to the drugstore where he had left the prescription, and he paid the druggist a dollar for the box of pills for Jock. He left and trotted the short distance to the bus station. He had to wait for a woman with three children to get her tickets and ask what time the bus got to Knoxville. When the woman and her three moved away he gave the man at the window $1.60 for the two tickets to Bessemer. "When does it come?" he asked.

"'Bout two hours."

Chris went outside and stood on the side of the road till the traffic was clear, then he scurried across to the taxi stand where the same man was wearing the same hat pulled down over his eyes.

"Mister, I want to go get my grandfather. He's out in the woods by the highway and he's sick." He held up three one-dollar bills. "And I got the money, and I got the money!"

13 ....

The wheels of the gitaway box made a grating, grinding, crunching sound as they rolled over bits and pieces of rock and rubble scattered along the edge of the cracked and weathered concrete roadbed of the old highway running south out of Bessemer. The tread of the little tires was long since gone and the rims were becoming ripple-notched, and the axle wobbled now and again when the wheels hesitated at an oversized rock.

The box itself was scratched and scarred and the bright lavender paint had weathered and washed and faded to a bleached-out gray, and the socket was loose where the handle fitted on. But the solid frame held firm and sturdy, the side hinged open and shut as smoothly now as it did the day Jock put it together, and not a single screw had worked free. Its remaining contents were securely nestled in crannies and cubbyholes, and the bumper sticker that proclaimed See Rock City still clung to the back where Jock had fixed it.

At the railroad crossing the box click-clack rumbled over the tracks and down the gentle slope on the other side. It moved on by the barren ground and shambles of where a place once proudly calling itself the Peacock Inn used to be but now was no more. It passed dirt-fronted houses whose faded paint and weathered boards mutely testified to the despair of their occupants, owners or renters, who could no longer cope with the polluted dust blown up by traffic and who seemed to accept the sound of cars going by as the appropriate background for their surrender.

Beyond the final edge of town, the gitaway box left the hard pavement and now made narrow tracks of its own on the grass and gravel shoulder of the road. Its noise was barely a scraping sound as it rolled on the outer side of the hedgerow fence encircling what the huge sign called Lakewood Estates, mansionlike houses with rolling, sprawling green lawns neatly kept, with huge oaks whose junctures of trunk and earth were left precisely wild, with curving driveways almost as wide as the access road leading from the highway.

And beyond, open country.

Chris pulled steadily on the gitaway box handle. "I hope you're not mad at me, Paw-paw, for what I did back yonder."

Jock kept easy pace. "Naw, boy, I ain't mad. Paw-paw couldn't be mad for you doin' what you done. Put out, maybe, for you not tellin' me what you was of a mind to do—but naw, sir, I ain't mad."

"I didn't go to do it that way. I *really* didn't. When I got to Bardock City, I did thumb. And one truck stopped, but he wouldn't take me. And when I figured out what to do, it was too late to ask."

"I reckon," Jock said, "I'd of spoke against it, if you'd of asked." He took a hitch at his belt and flexed his arm. He'd have done more than spoken against it, he remembered, he'd have kept the boy with him, wouldn't have sent him wandering off in the first place. They'd have camped right there by the stream, fished if they could, stayed a day or maybe two, long enough for him to get his strength back.

He had watched the boy out of sight, knowing till the final disappearance that he had done right sending him off. But once he could no longer see him, he had wanted him back, had called himself an addle-brained old fool for so much as thinking that the boy could hitchhike his way to Bucksville when he didn't know where it was, could find Aunt Jessie's house and bring her there. Had he felt up to it, he would have traipsed off after him, calling till Chris heard.

But he had not felt up to it. And after a while, when he knew the boy was well on his way to Bardock City, wherever it was, he sat down and slouched against the trunk of a hickory tree. And there he had fitfully dozed through the morning when the shadows were drawing closer to the tree, and through the afternoon and evening when they were going away from it again. By the time full dusk came, blending all the shadows into gray, when the ache in his arm was dulled and the tightness in his chest had eased, he had forced himself to believe Chris was on his way and would get there and in time would return. He had even convinced himself the return would be the following morning. And once he believed that, he got up and boiled water for coffee and for soaking dried prunes and apples. That night he had slept soundly, so soundly that he had been awake only long enough to heat what was left in the pot and eat the last two slices of dried bread with the last slice of cheese between them when he heard a car pull off the highway onto the shoulder. The boy had come scrambling and crashing through the underbrush, calling his name. He had grabbed him and held him close, listening as Chris told him how he had worked to get the money for the medicine and the bus tickets and the taxi ride, and wasn't Paw-paw glad they didn't have to walk the rest of the way to Bucksville.

The taxi driver had followed and stood uncertainly to the side, listening and wondering. "I'm the boy's gran'pa," Jock said. "Me an' him done come a long way."

"I don't know nothin' about that," the man had said, "but I heard talk last night about a young'un goin' around, cuttin' grass an' lookin' for work. Figured it was him when he asked the fare yesterday an' come with the money just now." He scratched his head, this time pushing his hat way back. "Mister," he had said, "I don't know where kids like this'un come from, but if I knowed, me an' the missus'd go grab off half a dozen."

When he had taken Jock and Chris and the gitaway box back to Bardock City, he'd charged only $1.95. "Wasn't more'n three mile out an' three back," he said, "an' never mind what the speedometer said. It was busted. Better get it fixed 'fore I get took on a long trip." So there'd been enough money left over to buy each a bowl of hot soup and a grilled-cheese sandwich and a glass of milk. Afterward, the bus ride had been short and pleasant.

"Naw, boy," Jock said, "I ain't truly put out. You done well."

Chris wiped the back of his hand across his face. "Maybe if I'd told somebody yesterday you were sick, they'd have helped."

"You done just right, boy. Made Paw-paw prouder'n a hound pup treein' his first coon." He looked down at the youngster. "Your pa'd of been proud, I just know it."

They walked on, and now they were two miles out of the city, past Williben Junction and the ramshackle John Grinson's blacksmith shop that wasn't a blacksmith shop now but a rundown motor tuneup place. "Your pa worked in that place back when ol' Frank Grinson run it, Frank, he was John's gimpy brother what was always fightin' 'cause he said he got them legs hurt in the war, but folks around that knowed him knowed better."

"I still think about daddy—mommy too."

"Reckon it's right you do," Jock said. "You don't want to never forget 'em; they gave life to you."

"Do you think about them, Paw-paw?"

"A heap, boy. But this here trip was good for us, for both of us. Me an' you, we had us a big hurt up yonder, big as the good Lord ever means for anybody to have. But travelin' the way we done, that was like puttin' fat on a burn, took the sting out."

They walked on, and now they were five miles out of the city, going past Pinehaven Lake and the aging picnic tables spread out under towering pines. "That's where your pa used t' sneak off an' court Stella," Jock said. "Her 'quaintances didn't like it 'cause Andy'd had that trouble with the law. But he done right by her, marryin' her an' then havin' you."

"Maybe we can come here someday and you can show me where they'd go."

"An' maybe fish," Jock said. "We'll sure do it, boy."

They walked on and on, and now they were seven miles away from Bessemer, and off to the left was a dirt road, the loose gravel that once covered it now scattered mostly to the sides, but with little mounds of it in the center. A hundred yards off the highway and back from the dirt road the freshly charred remains of a building stood gaunt and shadowy in the early shade of dusk. Jock stopped and stared at it. "'Member me tellin' you to come lookin' for Willie Timmons's store? Well, boy, that was it. An' if you'd of done like I said, you mightn' never of found Aunt Jessie."

They left the paved highway and took to the dirt and gravel route. "Paw-paw, maybe Aunt Jessie won't have a place for us to stay. Maybe we'll have to keep on campin' out."

"Never mind, boy, Aunt Jessie'll make do. Her an' R. T. ain't got much place, that an' all them kids gets the house a little crowdy, but me an' you'll tote our own load, now don't you fret. It ain't like we aim to live with 'em always."

"If we don't live with them, what'll we do?"

"They's an ol' run-down shack next to their'n. Ain't nobody lived there for longer'n I can think. Maybe we'll get us some scrap lumber an' fix it up for me an' you. Maybe even one of their'n can stay with us."

They came to a bend in the road and through the half-overgrown fields of the countryside they could see the big old house with the wide veranda and the scraggly grass yard a good two hundred yards away, the house where Aunt Jessie lived.

"Paw-paw, there's something I've been meaning to ask."

"What's that, boy?"

"The gitaway box," the boy said. "I want it, I want to keep it when we get there. You know, to put things in, like clothes and that little box we brought, and the slingshot, and knife that man gave me."

"Boy, I wouldn' let nobody else in the whole wide world have it 'cept you. Me an' you'll clean it up an' paint it all over an' maybe put little legs on it, an' you'd have the best plunder chest ever."

Jock put his hand on the worn handle and Chris kept his there, too, and they pulled the gitaway box the rest of the way together.

Ready For More Great Reading From David C. Cook?

FOR AGES 9-14

Dear Angie, Your Family Is Getting A Divorce

Mom and Dad's marriage problems make junior-high growing pains even worse.

BY CAROL NELSON

Angie's world seems to fall apart when her parents announce a trial separation. How can this happen to a Christian family? How will they cope? Is it her fault?

Dear Angie, Your Family is Getting a Divorce **#52464—$2.50**

The Gitaway Box

An old man and a boy run away from home...and make some surprising discoveries

BY HILARY MILTON

Threatened with being sent to institutions, a boy and his grandfather set out on foot to find a new home...an experience that forces the boy "to grow up" and helps him claim his grandfather's deep faith in God for himself.

The Gitaway Box **#52431—$2.95**